PENGUI

KUSAMAKURA

NATSUME SŌSEKI (1867-1916), one of Japan's most influential modern writers, is widely considered the foremost novelist of the Meiji era (1868-1912). Born Natsume Kinnosuke in Tokyo, he graduated from Tokyo University in 1893 and then taught high school English. He went to England on a Japanese government scholarship, and when he returned to Japan, he lectured on English literature at Tokyo University and began his writing career with the novel *I Am a Cat*. In 1908 he gave up teaching and became a full-time writer. He wrote fourteen novels, including *Botchan* and *Kokoro*, as well as haiku, poems in the Chinese style, academic papers on literary theory, essays, and autobiographical sketches. His work enjoyed wide popularity in his lifetime and secured him a permanent place in Japanese literature.

MEREDITH MCKINNEY holds a Ph.D. in medieval Japanese literature from the Australian National University in Canberra, where she teaches at the Japan Centre. She taught in Japan for twenty years and now lives near Braidwood, New South Wales. Her other translations include *Ravine and Other Stories* by Furui Yoshikichi, *The Tale of Saigyo*, and, for Penguin Classics, *The Pillow Book of Sei Shōnagon*.

NATSUME SŌSEKI

Kusamakura

Translated with an Introduction and Notes by
MEREDITH MCKINNEY

PENGUIN BOOKS

PENGUIN BOOKS

Published by the Penguin Group

Penguin Group (USA) Inc., 375 Hudson Street, New York, New York 10014, U.S.A.
Penguin Group (Canada), 90 Eglinton Avenue East, Suite 700, Toronto, Ontario, Canada M4P 2Y3
(a division of Pearson Penguin Canada Inc.)
Penguin Books Ltd, 80 Strand, London WC2R 0RL, England
Penguin Ireland, 25 St Stephen's Green, Dublin 2, Ireland (a division of Penguin Books Ltd)
Penguin Group (Australia), 250 Camberwell Road, Camberwell, Victoria 3124, Australia
(a division of Pearson Australia Group Pty Ltd)
Penguin Books India Pvt Ltd, 11 Community Centre, Panchsheel Park, New Delhi-110 017, India
Penguin Group (NZ), 67 Apollo Drive, Rosedale, North Shore 0632, New Zealand
(a division of Pearson New Zealand Ltd)
Penguin Books (South Africa) (Pty) Ltd, 24 Sturdee Avenue, Rosebank,
Johannesburg 2196, South Africa

Penguin Books Ltd, Registered Offices:
80 Strand, London WC2R 0RL, England

This translation first published in Penguin Books 2008

3 5 7 9 10 8 6 4

Translation and introduction copyright © Meredith McKinney, 2008
All rights reserved

LIBRARY OF CONGRESS CATALOGING-IN-PUBLICATION DATA
Natsume, Soseki, 1867–1916.
[Kusamakura. English]
Kusamakura / Natsume Soseki ; translated with an introduction by Meredith McKinney.
p. cm.—(Penguin classics)
ISBN 978-0-14-310519-0
1. McKinney, Meredith, 1950–   II. Title.
PL812.A8K813 2008
895.6'342—dc22   2007024784

Printed in the United States of America
Set in Sabon

Contents

Introduction by MEREDITH MCKINNEY   vii

A Note on the Translation   xv

Acknowledgments   xvii

Suggestions for Further Reading   xix

KUSAMAKURA   1

Notes   147

Introduction

Kusamakura (1906) is an extraordinary work, written at an extraordinary time in Japan's history, when the nation was tumbling headlong into the twentieth century and toward its "modern miracle," even as its traditional past everywhere still haunted it. *Kusamakura* was conceived out of this double consciousness and embodies it in fascinating ways. It is very much a novel of its historical moment, a literary experiment that was as new and exciting as the great experiment that was Meiji-era Japan.

Until 1868, when the Meiji era began, Japan had maintained a fiercely isolationist policy that kept it culturally and politically intact for centuries. When the nation finally chose, after a brief internal struggle, to submit to external pressure and open its doors, this largely untouched world of "old Japan" was suddenly subjected to violent upheavals, with the immediate rush to modernize and Westernize. In *Kusamakura* the powerful and inexorable transforming impetus that was impelling Japan out of its past and into a very different future is embodied in the image of the steam train of the final scene "hurtling blindly into the darkness ahead" with its freight of hapless passengers, an image of the sinister "serpent of civilization" that carries the novel off into its open-ended future. In this final scene the steam train is bearing away men who are leaving to fight in the Russo-Japanese War of 1904–5, a war that had just drawn to its victorious end when Natsume Sōseki wrote this work. Though written at the height of the nationalistic fervor that followed this victory, the novel portrays the war as a bloodbath whose distant echo of guns has penetrated even the idyllic peace of a mountain village that is otherwise virtually untouched by the modern world. Unlike so many of his contemporaries, Sōseki had a complex and deeply uneasy relationship with the new modernity.

Kusamakura is at odds not only with the generalized euphoric embrace of modernity but also more specifically with the contemporary trends in Japan's modern literature. Japanese prose writers had rushed to reject the earlier traditions and set about forging a new literature modeled on Western concepts of the novel. The Naturalism of nineteenth-century French writers such as Émile Zola provided the model for works that aimed at a gritty realism and an emphasis on human entanglements. Sōseki, however, instinctively rebelled against this unthinking rejection of Japan's native literary tradition and the focus on the more squalid aspects of the human world. *Kusamakura* is his attempt at an answer to this literary vogue, reaching back into Japan's literary past to bring its riches to bear on the possible evolution of the new Japanese novel.

Sōseki was in an ideal position to seek a new literary synthesis of "East and West." Natsume Kinnosuke (Sōseki was his nom de plume) was born in 1867, the final year of the old regime, into a family of minor bureaucrats whose fortunes declined rapidly with the onset of the Meiji era. A late and unwanted child in a large family, he was adopted the following year by a childless couple, then returned nine years later, when the couple divorced, to his parents (whom he believed to be his grandparents). This loveless and lonely childhood marked him with a sense of estrangement and dislocation that haunted him through his adult years and that echoed the dislocations and questioning of identity that were hallmarks of Meiji-era Japan.

Sōseki's education too epitomized the split consciousness of his time. As a child, he was given a traditional education with a strong grounding in the Chinese and Japanese classics—his love of this rich literary tradition is a constant presence in *Kusamakura* and to a lesser extent in everything he wrote. A bright student, he later chose to concentrate on the study of English, which was an important prerequisite for a scholarly career, and at Tokyo University he majored in English literature, but the classics remained his first and deepest love. Here again he was haunted by a sense of dislocation between his inheritance and the world in which he found himself, which he embraced with an unwilling fascination. Where others were throwing themselves indiscriminately into the huge experiment of modernization, with a largely uncritical adulation of Western culture and its values, Sōseki studied it carefully and was impressed and intrigued by it but found himself unable to embrace it wholeheartedly. He belonged to neither world and to both, and this uneasy, complex identity informs his writing, making him a uniquely Meiji voice.

Once he graduated, Sōseki took up a series of teaching posts, although he felt himself to be more scholar than teacher. During the following years he moved first to a school in Matsuyama in Shikoku (where he married) and then to Kumamoto in Kyūshū. While there he paid a visit to the nearby hot spring village of Oama, which evidently formed the basis for his depiction of Nakoi in *Kusamakura*. Kumamoto was far from Tokyo, and such small villages at the turn of the century would still have preserved virtually intact the traditional Japan that was Sōseki's first inheritance and love. Perhaps the visit to Oama stayed in his imagination as the epitome of a brief journey into the apparently idyllic past, to set against the stresses and alienation of life in modern Japan. Although he had not yet begun to write, Sōseki was already absorbing themes and material for his later novels.

In 1900 the Japanese government provided Sōseki with a scholarship to study in England for two years, part of its design to send promising scholars abroad to bring back an informed understanding of key aspects of Western civilization. Unwillingly, Sōseki set sail for London, leaving behind his wife and baby daughter. The two years that followed were probably the unhappiest of his life. He was poor, he was intensely lonely, and he found nothing to love about the English or their way of life. England was aesthetically depressing for him—we can guess that the occasional criticisms of England scattered throughout *Kusamakura* echo the author's own sentiments. He took meager lodgings, spoke to few people other than his landlady, and spent most of his time reading in his room, since he had failed to enroll himself in any formal course of study. He read widely, not only in literature but also in art, philosophy, and science, all the while fervently attempting to formulate for himself a position that would allow him to be true to his "Japaneseness" in relation to this very different culture whose influence was so rapidly transforming Japan.

Yet even in the unhappy depths of his time in London, Sōseki never simply rejected the West, as a less diligently honest and inquiring person might have done. He found much that earned his respect, particularly in the realms of literature and art. *Kusamakura* is on one level a working-through of his complex and ambivalent relationship to Western culture. A quotation from Shelley's poem "To a Skylark" springs as readily to the protagonist's mind as a quotation from Chinese poetry, and the novel's frequent long digressions are often devoted to much the same sort of pondering on the relative merits of the two cultures as would have filled Sōseki's thoughts and notebooks during his lonely days in London. These questions remained of intense concern to him throughout his life. To such questions there could be no final answer. *Kusamakura* can be read as a journey through this terrain, a philosophical novel that delicately probes important propositions about the two cultures but necessarily draws no conclusions.

When Sōseki returned to Japan in 1903, he was required to take up a post teaching at the First National College in Tokyo, as well as lecturing in English literature at Tokyo University. His nerves, never strong, had been brought close to the breaking point by the London years. Partly, it seems, as a way of soothing and entertaining himself, he began to write fiction. In 1905 the gently humorous novel *I Am a Cat* (*Wagahai wa neko de aru*) was serialized in a magazine and proved immediately popular. *Botchan* followed in 1906, sealing his reputation as a new and exciting novelist. *Kusamakura* appeared in the same year.

By this time his four-year teaching term was almost over, and Sōseki's fame as a novelist was now such that the *Asahi* newspaper offered him a monthly salary to serialize all future novels. To everyone's astonishment, Sōseki accepted, turning his back on a likely professorship and honorable academic career. From 1907 until his death ten years later, at the end of 1916, he was a professional writer. During this time he wrote steadily, at the rate of around one novel a year, the works that would establish him as the foremost author of his time and the revered father of modern Japanese literature, whose works are still read and loved today.

Kusamakura forms a kind of bridge between the first, lighthearted novels and the works Sōseki wrote as an established and professional author, such novels as *And Then* (*Sore kara*, 1909), *The Wanderer* (*Kōjin*, 1912), and *Kokoro* (1914), in which loneliness and introspection have become the dominant theme and tone. For all its seriousness of purpose, *Kusamakura* carries through from the early novels a delightful lightness and a wry, gently ironic humor. It is, however, in almost every way an anomaly, in terms both of Sōseki's work and of the modern Japanese novel. Written when Sōseki was in his late thirties, balanced at the edge of a professional writing career, and self-consciously placing itself at the beginning of a new century, with Japan balanced on the edge of its own very different future, *Kusamakura* embodies a moment when Sōseki, and Japanese literature, paused to look backward and forward and to play with possibilities.

It was, Sōseki said, written in the space of a week. The claim seems hardly credible, yet a certain intensity and tightness of interwoven motifs certainly suggest concentrated and even feverish writing. By any standard, the prose is extraordinarily polished—if it was indeed written in a week, it stands as supreme testimony to Sōseki's mastery of style and language.

The discursive passages often rise to a sonorous ornateness that echoes the classical Chinese-influenced prose of an earlier era, replete with the parallelisms and phrasal balancing of Chinese literary writing. This style was already dated and somewhat difficult in its time; to modern readers, it is sometimes almost impenetrable. The descriptive passages, on the other hand, are elegantly poetic in the best Japanese tradition. In style as well as in content, Sōseki was self-consciously experimenting with new forms by drawing on old.

In a brief piece entitled "My *Kusamakura*" (*Yo ga* Kusamakura), Sōseki stated that his aim had been to write "a haiku-style novel." Previous novels, he said, were works in the manner of the *senryū*, the earthier version of haiku that looks at everyday human life with a wryly humorous eye. "But it seems to me," he wrote, "that we should also have the haiku-style novel that lives through beauty." He had written *Kusamakura* "in a spirit precisely opposite to the common idea of what a novel is. All that matters [in this work] is that a certain feeling, a feeling of beauty, remain with the reader. I have no other objective. Thus, there is no plot, and no development of events."

The plot is certainly exiguous. A nameless young artist sets off on a purposely aimless walking trip across the mountains to the remote village of Nakoi, where he stays at a hot spring inn and indulges in an artistic experiment: to observe all he sees, humans included, with a detached, aesthetic eye, in the manner of the artists and poets of old. The novel traces this process, recording his experiences in the first person, most particularly his encounter with the startling, intriguing, and beautiful Nami, the daughter of the establishment. The scene is perfectly set for a romantic entanglement—but nothing happens. In the final chapter, he joins Nami and her family as they travel by boat down to the town, returning himself and us to modern civilization. The novel flirts with plot as Nami flirts with the young man, never intending any serious development, intent on its own ends. Nami, the center of the novel, is (as Sōseki pointed out) the still point, the enigma, around which the artist moves, watching and pondering the highly dramatized series of images of herself that she proffers him. When at last he glimpses in her a moment of unguarded pity, it completes the "picture" he has been working toward in his mind, and with it the novel.

Kusamakura embodies its own experiment: it sets off with the artist to explore just how and to what extent the serene beauty that was the artistic ideal of the past might be achievable in terms of a twentieth-century Japanese consciousness and its artistic products. The lofty "unhuman" and "nonemotional" approach to which this artist aspires—the ideal of a cool and uninvolved aesthetic response to all experience—can only be compromised by experience itself, and this is indeed what happens in the course of the novel. Yet the original aim of this experimental journey, to attempt to keep "beauty" as the central focus, is retained through all its testings. *Kusamakura* succeeds in embodying difficult balances.

Like Sōseki, this artist is deeply imbued with an understanding of and respect for the traditions he has inherited, yet he is an artist "in the Western style," a modern man with a wide-ranging grasp of Western culture. He has returned out of the very different present to bask for a brief time in the old world of beauty and serenity that the village of Nakoi embodies, but he necessarily brings with him the outsider's eye of modern Japan, with all its yearnings and confusions and ironic knowledge of the wider world. The village, still precariously maintained in a "timeless past," is slowly revealed as a place whose dream is disturbed by the distant violent disruptions of the modern world. Like the artist with his problematic outsider's vision, Nami, the central embodiment of the beauty that he encounters and with which he must come to terms, is also "returned" from the outside world, and her confusions and complexities cannot be contained by the village or by any simple portrayal of her. At the end of the novel she remains essentially elusive.

The artist in fact never succeeds in painting Nami (whose name itself means "beauty"), that potential amalgam of

Western and Japanese artistic vision that has haunted him, and after the experiment of *Kusamakura* Sōseki likewise did not pursue his vision of the new novel that takes "beauty" as its central aim and premise. He seems to have abandoned his brave hopes for this "haiku-style novel" as Japan's answer to the realistic novel of Western-style Naturalism. Honesty about the truths of modern experience compelled him to focus his subsequent novels on the contemporary world of the "new Japan" and to explore its lonely consciousness.

Kusamakura undoubtedly does achieve its aim of impressing the reader with a pervasive sense of beauty. Its intensely visual writing gives us a rich experience of the world filtered through the double aesthetic consciousness of "East and West" that the artist-protagonist embodies. Woven through is the voice of the first-person consciousness that experiences and comments, thinking through implications, sometimes opinionated and posturing, a gently ironic yet deeply serious voice that both is and is not the voice of Sōseki himself. This sometimes difficult discursive style (which holds echoes of Western writers Sōseki admired, such as Laurence Sterne) brings a strong philosophical dimension to the work. The constant digressions are also a foil to any latent urge toward plot. They hold the reader firmly inside the terms of the novel: to explore experience rather than be swept along by it. We, like the protagonist and Sōseki himself, emerge from this journey with its larger questions left unanswered, but with a wealth of fresh understanding and experience that has made the journey well worthwhile.

MEREDITH McKINNEY

A Note on the Translation

It is, of course, impossible to reproduce adequately in English the effect of Sōseki's prose, particularly the frequent passages of elevated diction and parallel syntax in the Chinese style, which contrast with sections, such as the farcical barbershop scene of Chapter 5, that draw on the alternative tradition of a comic and "vulgar" mode. In much of *Kusamakura*, Sōseki's style is consciously elegant and literary, carefully distinguishing itself from the modern Japanese of the Naturalist writers of his day (although in other ways the writing is contemporary and even innovative in the history of the modern novel). I have attempted to preserve its tone with a rather more old-fashioned literary language than contemporary written English. My primary aim has been to give some sense of the elegance of the Japanese, although reproducing its beauty is impossible.

Most of the novel is written in the present tense. Since English, unlike Japanese, cannot sustain occasional shifts to past-tense narration, I have chosen to retain the present tense throughout, in order to reproduce the effect of the journey's open-ended experiment that asks the reader to experience the protagonist's moment-by-moment feelings and thoughts.

A final word about the title. This novel was previously translated by Alan Turney with the title *The Three-Cornered World*, a reference to the quirky nature of the artist found in Chapter 3. The Japanese title, *Kusamakura* (literally "grass pillow"), is a traditional literary term for travel, redolent of the kind of poetic journey epitomized by Bashō's *Narrow Road to the Deep North*. I have chosen to retain the original Japanese title.

Acknowledgments

My thanks to the Australian National University's Japan Centre, which provided me with a haven as a Visiting Fellow while I worked on this translation.

Nobuo Sakai generously spared me his precious time to read through the translation and carefully check for errors.

I also owe a debt of gratitude to Elizabeth Lawson, whose perceptive comments and suggestions helped the manuscript to achieve its final form.

Suggestions for Further Reading

OTHER WORKS BY NATSUME SŌSEKI

Brodey, Inger Sigrun; Ikuo Tsunematsu; and Sammy I. Tsunematsu, trans. *My Individualism and the Philosophical Foundations of Literature*. Tokyo: Tuttle, 2005.

Cohn, Joel, trans. *Botchan*. Tokyo: Kodansha International, 2007.

Ito, Aiko, and Graeme Wilson, trans. *I Am a Cat*. Tokyo: Tuttle, 2002.

McClellan, Edwin, trans. *Grass on the Wayside*. Tokyo: Tuttle, 1971.

———, trans. *Kokoro*. Washington, D.C.: Gateway Editions, 2003.

Rubin, Jay, trans. *Sanshiro*. Ann Arbor: Michigan Classics in Japanese Studies. Michigan University, 2002.

WORKS ON NATSUME SŌSEKI

Beangcheon, Yul. *Natsume Sōseki*. London: Macmillan, 1984.

Brodey, Inger Sigrun. "Natsume Sōseki and Laurence Sterne: Cross-Cultural Discourse on Literary Linearity." *Comparative Literature* 50, no. 3 (Summer 1998), 193-219.

Brodey, Inger Sigrun, and Sammy I. Tsunematsu. *Rediscovering Natsume Sōseki*. London: Global Books, 2001.

Iijima, Takehisa, and James M. Vardaman, Jr., eds. *The World of Natsume Sōseki*. Tokyo: Kinseido, 1987.

McLellan, Edwin. *Two Japanese Novelists, Sōseki and Toson*. Tokyo: Tuttle, 2004.

Miyoshi, Masao. *Accomplices of Silence: The Modern Japanese Novel*. Berkeley: University of California Press, 1974.

Rubin, Jay. "The Evil and the Ordinary in Sōseki's Fiction." *Harvard Journal of Asiatic Studies* 46, no. 2 (December 1986), 333–52.

Turney, Alan. "Sōseki's Development as a Novelist Until 1907 with Special Reference to the Genesis, Nature and Position in His Work of *Kusa Makura*." *Monumenta Nipponica* 41, no. 4 (Winter 1986), 497–99.

Yiu, Angela. *Chaos and Order in the Works of Natsume Sōseki*. Honolulu: University of Hawaii Press, 1998.

Kusamakura

CHAPTER 1

As I climb the mountain path, I ponder—

If you work by reason, you grow rough-edged; if you choose to dip your oar into sentiment's stream, it will sweep you away. Demanding your own way only serves to constrain you. However you look at it, the human world is not an easy place to live.

And when its difficulties intensify, you find yourself longing to leave that world and dwell in some easier one—and then, when you understand at last that difficulties will dog you wherever you may live, this is when poetry and art are born.

The creators of our human world are neither gods nor demons but simply people, those ordinary folk who happen to live right there next door. You may feel the human realm is a difficult place, but there is surely no better world to live in. You will find another only by going to the nonhuman; and the nonhuman realm would surely be a far more difficult place to inhabit than the human.

So if this best of worlds proves a hard one for you, you must simply do your best to settle in and relax as you can, and make this short life of ours, if only briefly, an easier place in which to make your home. Herein lies the poet's true calling, the artist's vocation. We owe our humble gratitude to all practitioners of the arts, for they mellow the harshness of our human world and enrich the human heart.

Yes, a poem, a painting, can draw the sting of troubles from a troubled world and lay in its place a blessed realm before our grateful eyes. Music and sculpture will do likewise. Yet strictly speaking, in fact, there is no need to present this world in art. You have only to conjure the world up before you, and there you will find a living poem, a fount of song. No need to commit your thoughts to paper—the heart will already sing with a sweet inner euphony. No need to stand before your easel and limn with brush and paint—the world's vast array of forms and colors already sparkles within the inner eye. It is enough simply to be able thus to view the place we live, and to garner with the camera of the sentient heart these pure, limpid images from the midst of our sullied world. And so even if no verse ever emerges from the mute poet, even if the painter never sets brush to canvas, he is happier than the wealthiest of men, happier than any strong-armed emperor or pampered child of this vulgar world of ours—for he can view human life with an artist's eye; he is released from the world's illusory sufferings; he is able to come and go at ease in a realm of transcendent purity, to construct a unique universe of art, and thereby to destroy the binding fetters of self-interest and desire.

When I had lived in this world for twenty years, I understood that it was a world worth living in. At twenty-five I realized that light and dark are sides of the same coin; that wherever the sun shines, shadows too must fall. Now, at thirty, here is what I think: where joy grows deep, sorrow must deepen; the greater one's pleasures, the greater the pain. If you try to sever the two, life falls apart. Try to control them, and you will meet with failure. Money is essential, but with the increase of what is essential to you, anxieties will invade you even in sleep. Love is a happy thing, but as this happy love swells and grows heavy, you will yearn instead for the happy days before love came into your life. Splendid though he is, a cabinet minister must bear a million people on his shoulders; the weight of the whole nation rests heavy upon his back. If something is delicious, it goes hard not to eat it, yet if you eat a little you only desire more, and if you gorge yourself on it, it leaves you unpleasantly bloated. . . .

The vague drift of my thought is abruptly interrupted at

this point, when my right foot slips on a loose piece of sharp rock. I try to retain balance by shooting my left leg forward to compensate—and wind up landing on my bottom. Luckily, however, I have managed to come down on a wide boulder about three feet across. The painting box slung over my shoulder goes flying out from my side, but otherwise I escape any damage.

As I get back to my feet, my eyes take in the distant scene. To the left of the path soars a mountain peak, in shape rather like an inverted bucket. From foot to summit it is entirely covered in what could be either cypress or cedar, whose blue-black mass is striped and stippled with the pale pink of swaths of blossoming wild cherry. The distance is so hazy that all appears as a single wash of blurred shapes and colors. A little nearer, a single bald mountain rises above the others, lowering over me. Its naked flanks might have been slashed by the ax of some giant; they plunge with a ferocious steepness to bury themselves in the valley floor below. That solitary tree standing on the summit would be a red pine. The very sky between its branches is sharply defined. A few hundred yards ahead of me the path disappears, but the sight of a red-cloaked figure moving along in my direction far above suggests that a farther climb will bring me to that spot. The path is appallingly bad.

Of course the soil itself could quite easily be leveled; the trouble is that large rocks are embedded in it. Even were you to smooth the soil, there is no smoothing away these rocks, and even if the rocks were broken up, there would be no way to deal with the larger ones. They tower with serene indifference out of the broken earth of the track, innocent of any impulse to make way for the walker. Since they pay one no heed, there's nothing for it but to climb over them or go around them. And even where there is no rock, the walking is far from easy. The sides of the path rise steeply, while the center forms a deep depression; you could describe the six-foot width as gouged into a triangular shape whose deep apex lies down the middle of the path. Making one's way along it is more like fording a riverbed than walking a path. But it was never my intention to make this journey in haste, so I set off up the winding track, taking my time.

Suddenly a skylark bursts into song, directly beneath my feet. I gaze down into the valley but can see no sign of the creature. Only its voice rings out. The rapid notes pour busily forth, without pause. It's as if the whole boundless air were being tormented by the thousand tiny bites of a swarm of fleas. Not for an instant does the bird's outpouring of song falter; it seems it must sing this soft spring day right to its close, sing it into light and then sing it into darkness again. Up and up the skylark climbs, on and on—it will surely find its death deep in that sky. On and up it climbs, slipping at last into the clouds, and there perhaps its floating form dissolves, so that finally only that voice is left hanging in the far reaches of the heavens.

I turn a sharp rocky corner, then execute a swift, perilous swerve to the right to avoid a sudden drop into which a blind man would have tumbled headlong. Looking down, I see far below a vast yellow swath of wild mustard in flower. Perhaps, I think, this is the place that skylark would fall to in alighting— or no, perhaps it would instead soar upward out of that golden field. Then I imagine the tumbling skylark crossing paths with another as it rises. My final thought is that, whether falling or rising or crossing midair, the wild, vigorous song of the skylark would never for an instant cease.

Spring makes one drowsy. The cat forgets to chase the mouse; humans forget that they owe money. At times the presence of the soul itself is forgotten, and one sinks into a deep daze. But when I behold that distant field of mustard blossom, my eyes spring awake. When I hear the skylark's voice, my soul grows clear and vivid within me. It is with its whole soul that the skylark sings, not merely with its throat. Surely there's no expression of the soul's motion in voice more vivacious and spirited than this. Ah, joy! And to think these thoughts, to taste this joy—this is poetry.

Shelley's poem about the skylark immediately leaps to my

mind. I try reciting it to myself, but I can remember only two
or three verses. One of them goes

> We look before and after
> And pine for what is not:
> Our sincerest laughter
> With some pain is fraught;
> Our sweetest songs are those that tell of saddest
> thought.

Yes indeed, no matter how joyful the poet may be, he cannot
hope to sing his joy as the skylark does, with such passionate
wholeheartedness, oblivious to all thought of before and after.
In Chinese poetry one often finds suffering expressed as, for instance, "a hundredweight of sorrows," and similar expressions
can be seen in Western poetry too of course, but for the non-
poet, the poet's hundredweight may well be a mere dram or so.
It strikes me now that poets are great sufferers; they seem to
have more than double the nervous sensitivity of the average
person. They may experience exceptional joys, but their sorrows too are boundless. This being the case, it's worth thinking
twice before you become a poet.

The path continues level for a while, with the broadleaf forest
on the mountainside to my right, and down to the left the endless fields of mustard blossom. My feet occasionally tread down
a dandelion as I walk. Its sawtoothed leaves spread themselves
expansively in all directions, and at its center it nurses a nest of
golden balls. I turn to look back, regretful at having inadvertently trodden on it while my attention was held by the mustard blossom. But those golden balls are sitting there just as
before, still enshrined in their sawtoothed circle. What insouciant creatures they are! I return to my thoughts.

Sorrows may be the poet's unavoidable dark companion,
but the spirit with which he listens to the skylark's song holds
not one jot of suffering. At the sight of the mustard blossoms
too, the heart simply dances with delight. Likewise with dan-
delions, or cherry blossoms—but now I suddenly realize that

in fact the cherries have disappeared from sight. Yes, here among these mountains, in immediate contact with the phenomena of the natural world, everything I see and hear is intriguing for me. No special suffering can arise from simply being beguiled like this—at worst, surely, it is tired legs and the fact that I can't eat fine food.

But why is there no suffering here? Simply because I see this scenery as a picture; I read it as a set of poems. Seeing it thus, as painting or poetry, I have no desire to acquire the land and cultivate it, or to put a railway through it and make a profit. This scenery—scenery that adds nothing to the belly or the pocket—fills the heart with pleasure simply as scenery, and this is surely why there is neither suffering nor anxiety in the experience. This is why the power of nature is precious to us. Nature instantly forges the spirit to a pristine purity and elevates it to the realm of pure poetry.

Love may be beautiful, filial piety may be a splendid thing, loyalty and patriotism may all be very fine. But when you yourself are in one of these positions, you find yourself sucked into the maelstrom of the situation's complex pros and cons— blind to any beauty or fineness, you cannot perceive where the poetry of the situation may lie.

To grasp this, you must put yourself in the disinterested position of an outside observer, who has the leisurely perspective to be able to comprehend it. A play is interesting, a novel is appealing, precisely because you are a third-person observer of the drama. The person whose interest is engaged by a play or novel has left self-interest temporarily behind. For the space of time that he reads or watches, he is himself a poet.

And yet there's no escaping human feelings in the usual play or novel. The players suffer, rage, flail about, and weep, and the observer will find himself identifying with the experience, and suffering, raging, flailing, and weeping with them. The value of the experience may lie in the fact that there is nothing here of greedy self-interest, but unfortunately the other sentiments are more than commonly activated. Therein lies my problem with it.

There is no avoiding suffering, rage, flailing, and weeping in the world of humankind. Heaven knows I have experienced them myself in the course of my thirty years, and I have had enough of them by now. I find it exhausting to be forced to experience these same tired stimuli yet again through a play or novel. The poetry I long for is not the kind that provokes this type of vulgar emotion. It is poetry that turns its back on earthly desires and draws one's feelings for a time into a world remote from the mundane. No play, however brilliant, is free from human feelings. Rare is the novel that transcends questions of right and wrong. The characteristic of these works is their inability to leave the world behind. Particularly in Western poetry, based as it is on human affairs, even the most sublime poem can never aspire to emancipation from this vulgar realm. It is nothing but Compassion, Love, Justice, Freedom—such poetry never deals with anything beyond what is found in the marketplace of the everyday world. No matter how poetic it may be, its feet stay firmly on the ground; it has a permanent eye on the purse. No wonder Shelley sighed so deeply as he listened to the skylark.

Happily, in the poetry of the Orient there are works that transcend such a state.

> By my eastern hedge I pluck chrysanthemums,
> Gazing serenely out at the southern hills.[1]

Here we have, purely and simply, a scene in which the world of men is utterly cast aside and forgotten. Beyond that hedge there is no next-door girl peeping in; no friend is busy pursuing business deals among those hills. Reading it, you feel that you have been washed clean of all the sweat of worldly self-interest, of profit and loss, in a transcendental release.

> Seated alone in a deep bamboo grove
> I pluck my lute, I hum a melody.
> Nobody knows me here within this wood,
> Only the bright moon comes to shine on me.[2]

In these few lines, the poet has constructed the space of a whole other universe. The virtues of this universe are not those of contemporary novels such as *Hototogisu* or *Konjikiyasha*.[3] They are virtues equivalent to those of a luxurious sleep that releases a mind exhausted by the world of steamships and trains, rights and duties, morals and manners.

If such restorative sleep is a necessity in this dawning twentieth century of ours, then the poetry of transcendence must be a precious thing. Unfortunately, our poets today and their readers have all become infected by Western writers, and no more do they set off in a cheerful little boat upstream to a land of peace and tranquillity.[4] I am not a poet by profession, so my intention is not to preach the virtues of Wang Wei or Tao Yuanming to the modern world. It's just that, for myself, I find more healing for the heart in the delights of these poems than in the world of plays or dance parties. Such poetry gives me more pleasure than does *Faust* or *Hamlet*. This is precisely why I stroll these spring mountains now with painting box and tripod slung on my back. I long to breathe and absorb the natural world of Yuanming and Wang Wei's poetry, to loiter awhile in the realm of unhuman detachment. Call it a whim of mine.

I'm a human and belong to the world of humans, of course, so for me the unhuman can last only so long, no matter how much I may enjoy it. Yuanming too would not have spent the whole year simply gazing at the southern hills, and I imagine Wang Wei was not a man to sleep happily without a mosquito net in that bamboo grove of his. If he had chrysanthemums to spare, Yuanming would have sold the lot to the local flower shop, and Wang Wei would have done a deal with his greengrocer over the bamboo shoots. And I am no different. No matter how I love the skylark and the mustard blossom, my desire for the unhuman doesn't extend to bedding down in the mountains for the night. Even up here, after all, one meets with other humans. You will come across a fellow with his kimono skirts tucked up at the back and a cloth draped over his head, or a girl in a red wraparound, and even an occasional long-faced horse. You may breathe in the rare-fied air of this high altitude, deep among the miles of encircling cypress trees, yet it still holds the smell of man. Indeed, the place where I am headed tonight in search of peace across these mountains is the all-too-human realm of the hot spring inn at the village of Nakoi.

Nevertheless, how a thing looks depends on how you see it. "Listen to the bell," Leonardo da Vinci told his pupils. "It is a single sound, but you all hear it variously." A man or a woman too will appear very different depending on your point of view. Since I've come here to devote myself to the unhuman, this is the perspective on humans that I will take, and it is bound to be different from the view I would have from the midst of a life lived deep in the cramped little streets of the crowded world. Very well, granted that I can't altogether escape the realm of human feelings; at least I can probably maintain the light detachment experienced by the viewer of some classic Noh drama. The Noh drama, after all, has its human feelings. There is no guarantee you won't weep at a play like *Shichikiochi* or *Sumidagawa*.[5] But what we experience in these plays is the effect of three parts human feeling to seven parts art. The pleasure we gain from a Noh play springs not from any skill at presenting the raw human feelings of the everyday world but from clothing feeling "as it is" in layer upon layer of art, and in a kind of slowed serenity of deportment not to be found in the real world.

How would it be if I chose to view as actions in a Noh drama the events and people I meet with in the course of this journey? Of course I can't altogether do away with human feeling, but since this journey is essentially poetic in intent, it would be good to use the "unhuman" I seek to good effect and row its little boat as far upstream as possible. The southern hills and bamboo groves of those ancient poems are of a different nature, of course; nor can I treat humans quite as I do the skylark and mustard blossom; but my ideal is to approach that state as far as possible and do all I can to view humans from its vantage point. The poet Bashō, after all, found elegance even in the horse peeing by his pillow, and he composed a haiku about it.[6] Let me emulate him, then, and deal with the people I meet on this journey—farmer, townsman, village clerk, old man, or old woman—on the assumption that each is a small component figure in a landscape scroll painting. Unlike figures in a painting, of course, they will all be conducting their lives with a willful independence, but to treat them as a normal novelist would—to pursue the reasons behind their individual actions, delve into their psychological workings, and go into all the ins and outs of their human entanglements—would be merely vulgar. Of course they may move about. One can view the figures in a painting as moving forms, after all. But however much they move, those figures remain confined to the flat surface. Once you conceive of them as leaping out of the painting, you'll find them bumping up against you, and you'll become ensnared in the troublesome business of self-interested interactions with them. And the more troublesome they become, the less able you are to view them aesthetically. No, I shall aim to observe the people I meet from a lofty and transcendent perspective, and do my best to prevent any spark of human feeling from springing up between us. Thus, however animatedly they may move hither and yon, they won't find it easy to make the leap across to my heart; I will stand watching as before a picture, as they rush about inside it waving their arms. I can gaze with a calm and unflinching eye from the safe distance of three feet back. To express it another way: being free of self-interested motives, I will be able to devote all my energy to observing their actions from the point of view of Art. With no other thought in mind, I will be in a fine position to pass lofty judgment on the presence or absence of beauty in all I view. . . .

Just as I reach this conclusion, the sky grows suddenly ominous. The seething cloud that a little earlier began to loom overhead has quickly fractured and spread till all around me seems nothing but a sea of cloud, and now a gentle spring rain begins to fall. I have long since left the mustard blossom fields behind and am now high among mountains, but how close they are I cannot tell, owing to the veil of fine, almost mistlike rain. When a gust of wind from time to time parts the high clouds, I catch glimpses of the blackish shape of a high ridge off to my right. It seems that just across the valley from me runs a mountain range. Immediately to my right is the foot of another mountain. An occasional pine or some such tree appears suddenly from deep within the dense misty rain; no sooner is it there than it is gone again. Weirdly, I find myself unable to distinguish whether the rain is shifting, or the tree, or my own dreamy vision.

The path has grown surprisingly broad and flat, and I have no difficulty in walking now, but my lack of rain gear makes me hurry on my way. The rain is dripping from my hat when I hear, about ten yards ahead, the tinkle of a little bell, and out of the rainy darkness emerges a packhorse driver.

"Would there be anywhere to rest around here?" I ask.

"There's a teahouse a mile on. You're pretty wet, aren't you?"

Still a mile to go, I think, as the driver's figure envelops itself in rain like some shadowy magic lantern form and becomes lost to sight once more.

I watch as the fine-grained rain gradually thickens to long continuous threads, each twisted by the wind. My *haori* has long since become saturated,[7] and the water has now penetrated my underwear, where it grows tepid from the heat of my body. It's an unpleasant sensation, and I tilt my hat low and step briskly out.

If I picture myself, a sodden figure moving in this vast ink-wash world of cloud and rain shot through diagonally with a thousand silver arrows, not as myself but as some other person, there's poetry in this moment. When I relinquish all thought of the self as is and cultivate the gaze of pure objectivity, then for the first time, as a figure in a painting, I attain a beautiful harmony with the natural phenomena around me. The instant I revert to thoughts of my distress at the falling rain and the weariness of my legs, I lose my place in the world of the poem or painting. I am as before, a mere callow

townsman. The swirling brushstrokes of cloud and mist are a
closed book to me; no poetic sentiment of falling blossom or
calling bird stirs my breast; I have no way of understanding
the beauty of my own self as it moves lonely as cloud and rain
among the spring mountains. . . .

To begin with, I tilt my hat and stride out. Later, I simply
walk with eyes fixed on my feet. In the end, I am plodding
unsteadily along, with shoulders hunched. The branches filling my vision sway in the blowing rain, which drives in re-
lentlessly from every direction upon the solitary traveler. This
is a bit *too* much of the unhuman for my taste!

CHAPTER 2

"Anyone there?" I call. There is no response.

Standing beneath the eaves, I peer in. The smoke-stained paper screen doors beyond the entrance area are firmly shut, and what lies within is invisible. Half a dozen forlorn pairs of rough straw sandals dangle from the eaves' rafters, swaying listlessly to and fro. Below them is a neat row of three boxes containing cheap cakes, with a scattering of small coins at their sides.

"Anyone there?" I cry again. Several plumped fowl, asleep atop a hand mill that is tucked in one corner of the entrance, awaken with a start and set up a raucous cackle. Beyond the threshold a clay hearth stands, wet and partly discolored by the rain that is still falling. Above it hangs a blackened tea-kettle, whether earthenware or metal I cannot tell. Happily, the fire in the hearth is lit.

Since there is no reply, I take the liberty of going on in and sit myself down on a bench in the entrance area. The fowl flap noisily down from their perch on the hand mill and hop up onto the matting of the raised floor. They might well walk right into the room beyond if the screen doors weren't standing in their way. The rooster gives a lusty crow, and the hen takes up the cry more softly. They seem to view my intrusive presence as they would some fox or dog. On the stool sits a smoker's tray, about as large as a two-quart measure. The coil of incense inside it is sending up a tranquil curl of smoke, as if oblivious to the passage of time. The scene has a simple serenity. The rain gradually eases.

After a while footsteps are heard from within, then one of

the grimy screen doors slides smoothly open. An old woman appears.

I have been expecting someone to emerge sooner or later. The fire in the hearth is lit, after all; coins lie scattered about the cake boxes; the incense is left nonchalantly burning. Someone must eventually appear. But this casual way of leaving the shop open and unattended is rather different from the city ways I'm used to. And to simply go in and make myself at home like this, despite receiving no answer to my call, and to sit there patiently waiting, feels a little like stepping into an earlier century than the twentieth. All this is intriguingly otherworldly, that "nonemotional" realm I aspire to. What's more, I take an immediate fancy to the face of the old woman who has emerged.

Two or three years ago I saw a Hōshō School production of the Noh play *Takasago*,[1] and I remember being struck by the beautiful tableau vivant it made. The old man, brushwood broom on his shoulder, walks five or six steps along the bridgeway leading to the stage, then turns slowly back to face the old woman behind him. That pose, as they stand facing each other, remains vividly before my eyes to this day. From where I was seated, the old woman's face was more or less directly facing me. Ah, how beautiful! I thought, and in that moment her expression burned itself like a photograph into my heart. The face before me now and that face are so intimately alike that the same blood might flow in both.

"I'm afraid I've come in and made myself at home."

"Not at all. I had no idea you were here."

"That was quite some rain, wasn't it?"

"You must have had hard going, with this unfortunate weather. My goodness, you certainly are wet! Let me get the fire going and dry things off for you."

"If you'd just build up that fire a little, I can stand beside it and dry off. I seem to have got rather cold sitting here."

"I'll get it going right away. How about a cup of tea?" She rises to her feet and chases the fowl away with a quick "Shoo!

Shoo!" Clucking indignantly, they scramble off the age-stained matting, trample through the cake boxes, and flee out to the road, the rooster depositing a dropping in one of the boxes as he goes.

"Here you are," says the old woman, reappearing in no time with a teacup on a tray made from a hollowed piece of wood. In the bottom of the cup, which is stained a blackish brown from years of tea, three plum blossoms have been casually sketched with a few quick brushstrokes.

"Have a cake." She fetches me a sesame twist and a ground-rice stick cake from one of the boxes the fowl trampled through. I look them over warily, wondering if I'll find the rooster dropping, but evidently it remains somewhere in the box.

The old woman pulls her kimono sleeves back up her arms with a cord looped over her sleeveless work jacket, then crouches down in front of the hearth fire. I take out my sketchbook and draw her profile as we talk.

"It's lovely and quiet here, isn't it?"

"Yes, just a little mountain village, as you can see."

"Do you get bush warblers singing?"[2]

"Yes indeed, you hear them every day. They sing in summer too around here."

"I'd love to hear one now. When none is singing, you really long to hear one."

"Unfortunately it's not the day for it. They've gone off somewhere to get out of the rain."

The hearth has meanwhile begun to emit a crackling sound, and suddenly a scarlet flame shoots up a foot or more into the air, sending out a rush of heat.

"Here you are then, come and warm yourself," she urges. "You must be cold." A column of blue smoke rises to meet the edge of the eave, where it thins and dissipates, leaving faint wisps trailing in under the wooden roof.

"Ah, this feels good. You've brought me back to life."

"The rain's cleared off nicely now. Look, you can see Tengu Rock."

The storm has resolutely swept across the section of mountain before us, in apparent impatience at the spring sky's timid clouds, and there, where the old woman points, a towering rock like a rough-hewn pillar now soars against the brilliant blue left in the storm's relentless wake. This must be Tengu Rock.

I gaze first at the rock, then back at the old woman, then finally I hold them both in my line of sight, comparing. As an artist, my mind contains only two old woman images—the face of the old woman of the Noh play and that of the mountain crone of Rosetsu's painting.[3] When I saw Rosetsu's painting, I understood the eerie power inherent in the ideal image of the old woman. This was a figure to set among autumn leaves, I thought, or beneath a cold moon. Seeing that Noh play at the Hōshō theater, on the other hand, I was astonished at how gentle her expression can be. That Old Woman mask could only have been created by a master carver, though unfortunately I failed to learn the artist's name. This portrayal brought out a rich, tranquil warmth in the image—something that would be not unfitting depicted on a gilt screen, say, or set against spring breezes and cherry blossoms. As this old woman stands here, bare-armed and drawn up to her full height, one hand shading her eyes while the other points into the distance, her figure seems to match the scene of the mountain path in spring better than does the rugged form of Tengu Rock beyond. I take up my sketchbook again, in the hope that she will hold the pose just a little longer, but at that moment she moves.

"You look in fine shape, I must say," I remark, as I idly hold the sketchbook toward the fire to dry it.

"Yes, praise be, I keep in good health. I can still use a sewing needle, and spin flax, and grind the dumpling flour."

I have a sudden desire to watch her at work at the hand mill, but since I can't very well request this, I change the subject. "Nakoi is a bit over two miles on from here, is that right?"

"Yes, it's close on two miles. You're heading for the hot spring, are you, sir?"

"I thought I might stay there for a bit, if it's not crowded. I'll see how I feel."

"Oh no, it won't be. Since the war began, the guests have dropped right off. It's as good as closed now."[4]

"That's odd. Well, perhaps they won't put me up there, then."

"No, they're happy to put up anyone who asks."

"There's only one place to stay, isn't there?"

"Yes, just ask for Shioda's, and you'll have no trouble finding it. It's hard to tell whether Mr. Shioda keeps it more as an inn or as his own country retreat."

"So it wouldn't matter to him if there weren't any guests, then."

"Is this your first visit, sir?"

"No, I came through once a long time ago."

The conversation flags. I open up my sketchbook again and peacefully set about sketching the chickens. Then, deep in the quietness, the soft clang of a distant horse bell begins to penetrate my ears. It sets up a rhythm inside my head that grows into a kind of tune. It's like the dreamy feeling of being half aware, as you doze, of the soft, insistent sound of a hand mill turning next door. I pause in my sketching to jot down on the side of the page

> Spring wind—
> in Izen's ears the sound
> of a horse's bell.[5]

I have already come across five or six horses on my way up the mountain, all of them elaborately girthed in the old style, and belled. They seemed scarcely to belong to the present world.

Before long the tranquil strains of a packhorse driver's song break through my poetic reveries of an unpeopled path winding on among empty mountains into the far depths of spring. There is something carefree within the plaintive sorrow of that singing voice, and it strikes my ears as might a song from a painting.

The driver's song
crossing Suzuka's far pass—
spring rain falling.[6]

Having jotted these words diagonally on the page, I realize it
is not in fact my own poem.[7]

"Someone else has come," remarks the old woman, half to
herself.

Since there is only one path across the mountains, all who
come and go must pass her teahouse. Each of those five or six
horses I've met would have come down the path, and climbed
back up it again, to these same murmured words. Here in this
tiny settlement, strewn blossom-deep wherever feet might
tread, down the years she has counted the bells, through the
changeless springs along the hushed and lonely road, till now
her hair is white with the years of counting. Turning over a
page, I write

The driver's song—
white hair untouched by color
spring draws to its end.

But the poem doesn't manage to express all I'm feeling; it will
need some further thought. Staring at the tip of my pencil, I
am pondering how I might combine the phrase "white hair"
with "age-old melody" and the theme words "the driver's
song," add a season word for spring, and put it all into a
haiku's seventeen syllables, when a loud voice cries "Hello
there!" and in front of the shop stands the packhorse driver
himself.

"Well, well, so it's you, Gen. You're off down to town
again, eh?"

"If you have anything you want from there, just let me
know and I'll bring it up for you."

"Well then, if you're passing through the Kaji-chō area,
could you bring me a Reigan Temple talisman for my daughter?"

"Right, I'll get one for you. Just one? Your Aki's made a fine marriage. It's a happy thing. Isn't that so?"

"Praise be, she wants for nothing in daily life. I suppose that's a happy thing, yes."

"Of course it is! Just compare her with the Nakoi girl."

"Yes, poor thing. And so good-looking too. Is she any better these days?"

"Nah, just the same as ever."

"What a shame!" The old woman heaves a sigh.

"A shame it is," Gen agrees, stroking his horse's nose.

The rain that has streamed out of that distant sky is still held pooled in every leaf and blossom of the luxuriantly branching cherry tree nearby, and a passing gust of wind chooses this moment to catch the tree off guard, so that it finds itself toppling the heavy drops down from their precarious home aloft, with a sudden shower of sound. Startled, the horse tosses its long mane up and down.

"Whoa there!" scolds Gen, his voice combining with the clanging of the horse's bell to break through my meditations.

"You know, Gen," the old woman goes on, "I can still see before my eyes the sight of her when she went off as a bride. Sitting there on the horse, in that lovely long-sleeved wedding kimono with the patterned hem, and her hair up in the *takashimada* style . . ."[8]

"Yes, she didn't go down by boat, did she. We used the horse. She stopped off here on her way through, I remember."

"That's right. The horse stopped under that cherry there, and just then there was a little flurry of falling petals. That splendid *takashimada* hair was all dotted with them."

I open my sketchbook again. This scene could be a painting, or a poem. I picture in my mind's eye the figure of the bride, imagine the scene as if it were before me. Pleased with myself, I jot down

> Praise be to the bride
> who rides across the mountains
> through blossoming spring.

The odd thing is that, although I can clearly picture her clothes and hair, and the horse and the cherry tree, I simply cannot visualize the bride's face. I try out this one and that, until suddenly the face of Ophelia in Millais's painting springs unbidden to my mind, fitting itself perfectly under the *takashimada* hair.[9] This won't do, I think, hastily dismantling my careful picture in order to start afresh. But though the clothes and hair, and the horse and cherry tree, all disappear instantly from the scene, the figure of Ophelia, floating, hands folded, down the stream, still hovers dimly in the depths of consciousness, like smoke that a ragged broom cannot quite manage to dispel from the air. I have a weird sense of something like foreboding, as if I have witnessed a comet suddenly trail its light across the sky.

"Right then, if you'll excuse me, I'll be off," says Gen.

"Drop in again on your way back through. I'm afraid all that rain will have made the Seven Bends difficult to get around."

"Yes, it's a bit hard going," Gen replies as he moves away. His horse sets off behind him. *Clang, clang* goes the bell.

"He's from Nakoi, is he?"

"Yes, his name's Genbei."

"He once led some bride over the pass on his horse?"

"When Shioda's daughter went down to the town as a bride, they put her on a white horse for the bridal procession, and she came along past here with Genbei on the lead rein. Good heavens, how time flies—it'll be five years ago this year."

One who laments her white hair only when she looks in a mirror must be accounted among the happy. This old woman, who first comprehends the swiftness of the turning wheel of Time as she counts off on bent fingers the passage of five years, must then surely be closer to the unworldly mountain immortals than to us humans.

"She would have made a beautiful sight. I wish I'd come to see."

The old woman gives a chuckle. "You can see her still. If

you call in at the hot spring inn, she'll be sure to come out and greet you."

"Aha, so she's in the village now, is she? If only she were still dressed in that wedding kimono with her hair up in the *takashimada*."

"She may well dress up for you if you ask."

I very much doubt this, but the old woman does seem remarkably serious. This is just the sort of situation that a journey undertaken in the spirit of artistic "nonemotion" needs to encounter to make it worthwhile.

"She's very like the Nagara maiden, actually," remarks the old woman.

"Her face, you mean?"

"No, I mean the way things turned out for her."

"Really? Who's this Nagara maiden?"

"The story goes that there was once a beautiful daughter of the village rich man, who went by the name of 'the Nagara maiden.'"

"Yes?"

"Well, my dear, two men went and fell in love with her at the same time."

"I see."

"Her days and nights were spent tossing in an agony over whether she should give her heart to the Sasada man or whether it should be the Sasabe man, and she was sorely torn between them, till finally she composed a poem that went:

> As the autumn's dew
> that lies a moment on the tips
> of the seeding grass,
> so do I know that I too must
> fade and be gone from this brief world.[10]

And then she threw herself into a pool and drowned."

Little could I have dreamed that I would find myself in such a poetic place, hearing from such a poetic figure this elegant, time-worn tale, told in such elegant language!

"You ought to take a look at the Nagara maiden's grave while you're on your way through. If you go a little over half a mile east from here, you'll find the old stone grave marker."

I immediately decide I will do just that.

The old woman continues, "The Nakoi girl had the same ill fortune of being loved by two men, you see. One was a man she met while she was off training in Kyoto. The other was the richest man in the local town."

"Aha, and which did she give her heart to?"

"She was set on marrying the man in Kyoto, but her parents, no doubt for their own good reasons, made her accept the local man."

"Well, it's a blessing she didn't have to end up throwing herself in a pool, isn't it."

"Ah, but . . . this man wanted her on account of her beauty and talent. He may have been very good to her for all I know, but she'd been forced into the marriage and apparently she never got along with him. The family seemed very worried about how it was all going. And then along came this war, and the bank where her husband worked went bankrupt. After that she came back home to Nakoi. People say all sorts of things about her—that she's heartless and unfeeling, and so on. She was always such a gentle, reserved girl, but these days she's apparently turning a bit wild. Every time Genbei comes through here, he tells me how worrying she is."

It would ruin my planned picture to hear any more. I feel rather as if I have at last stumbled upon the magic feather cloak that will turn me into a mountain immortal, only to have some heavenly being come along and demand that I return it.[11] To find myself dragged back down into the vulgar world again, after having braved the perils of those Seven Bends to arrive at this place at last, would destroy the whole point of my aimless journey. If you let yourself become involved with worldly gossip past a certain point, the stench of the human world seeps in through the pores of your skin, and its grime begins to weigh you down.

"This road goes straight through to Nakoi, doesn't it?"

I inquire, rising to my feet and tossing a small coin onto the table.

"If you take a shortcut by following the path down to the right from the Nagara maiden's gravestone, it's a quick half mile. The path's rough, but it's probably the better way for a young gentleman like yourself. . . . This is very generous payment, sir. . . . Take good care."

CHAPTER 3

The evening is a strange and unsettling one.

It is eight o'clock at night by the time I arrive at the inn, so even my sense of direction is somewhat confused, let alone my grasp of the layout of the house and the type of garden it has. I am taken along a very winding passageway of some sort, and finally shown into a small, six-mat-sized room. The place is quite unlike my memory of it from the previous visit. I have my dinner, take a bath, return to my room, and am sipping tea when the maid arrives and offers to lay out the bedding. The strange thing is that it is this same maid who has done everything since I arrived—answering the door to me, serving the evening meal, showing me to the bathhouse, and now laying out my bed. What's more, she has scarcely spoken a word, though she doesn't seem particularly countrified in her ways. Earlier I followed behind this girl as she wound along the endless passageway-cum-staircase to my room, a chastely knotted red obi around her waist and an old-fashioned oil taper in her hand, and then I followed the same obi and oil taper down the same passageway-cum-staircase, on and on, as she led me to the bathhouse, feeling almost as if I was a figure coming and going in a painting.

While serving my evening meal, she apologizes that I have to put up with a room normally used for other purposes, since the recent lack of guests means the guest rooms haven't been cleaned. Later, as she leaves after preparing the bedding, she says a gentle, slow "Good night" that has some human warmth to it. But after her footsteps have grown distant and vanished down the twisting corridor, all is hushed and still, and I am uncomfortably aware of the lack of any sense of human presence in the place.

I have had this experience only once before. It was the time I traveled across Bōshū province[1] from Tateyama and followed the coast around on foot between Kazusa and Chōshi. One night I stayed at a certain place along the road—I can't put it any more clearly, since both the name of the area and the name of the inn are now quite forgotten. In fact, I'm not even sure it was an inn where I stayed. It was a high-roofed house, containing only two women. I asked if they could put me up; the older woman said yes, and the younger invited me to follow her. We passed through a number of large, dilapidated rooms to the farthest room, on the mezzanine floor. Having mounted the three steps from the corridor, I was about to enter the room when a clump of bamboo leaning in under the eaves swayed in the evening breeze and brushed its leaves over me from shoulder to head, sending a chill down my spine. The balcony boards were rotting. I observed to the girl that in another year the bamboo shoots would penetrate the balcony and the room would become overwhelmed by bamboo, but her only response was to grin and leave.

That night I couldn't sleep for the rustling of the bamboo near my pillow. Opening the screen doors to the balcony, I looked out and discovered that the garden was a sea of grass. I let my eyes travel out over the scene through the bright summery moonlight; the grass flowed on into a great grassy hill beyond, without any intervening hedge or wall. Directly beyond the hill the breakers of the mighty ocean thundered in to menace the world of man. I didn't sleep a wink until dawn, and as I lay there grimly, hour upon hour inside the eerie tent of the mosquito net, I felt I had strayed into the gothic realm of those popular romantic tales of a previous era.

I have been on many journeys since then, but never again until this night in Nakoi have I had a similar experience.

Lying there on my back, I happen to open my eyes and notice hanging above the sliding doors a piece of calligraphy framed in red lacquer. Even from where I lie, I can clearly read the words: "Bamboo shadows sweep the stair, but no dust moves."[2] I can also make out that the signature seal gives the calligrapher's name as Daitetsu. Now I am in no way a connoisseur of calligraphy, but I have always loved the style of the Ōbaku Zen priest Kōsen. There's a lot to be said for the calligraphy of Ingen, Sokuhi, and Mokuan as well,[3] but Kōsen's writing is the most powerful and meticulous. Looking at these seven characters before me now, both the handling of the brush and the flow of the writing hand convince me that it must be the work of Kōsen. But this cannot be so, as the signature is Daitetsu. I consider the possibility that there might also have been a priest named Daitetsu in the Ōbaku sect at that time, but the paper looks far too new. It can surely only be a recent work.

I turn on my side. Now my eyes take in the painting of cranes by Jakuchū that hangs in the alcove.[4] Art being my line of work, I registered this as a superb piece when I first entered the room. Most of Jakuchū's works have a quite delicate coloration, but this crane is executed with a single defiant brushstroke. The featherlight, egg-shaped body poised jauntily on its single leg has a wonderful rightness to it, and the sense of nonchalant ease continues right down to the tip of the beak. Beside the alcove is a single shelf with a cupboard beyond. What is in the cupboard I cannot tell.

I slip into a peaceful sleep, into dream.

The Nagara maiden in her long-sleeved kimono is riding over the mountain pass on a white horse when suddenly the Sasada man and the Sasabe man leap out on her from either side and both begin to pull at her. The girl now suddenly becomes Ophelia, lying upon a drifting willow branch in the water's flow, singing beautifully. I pick up a long pole and race along the bank in search of a place from which to rescue her, but she floats away and is lost to sight, singing and smiling, apparently perfectly at ease. I stand calling desperately after her, the pole over my shoulder.

Then I awaken. My armpits are soaked with sweat. What an extraordinary jumble of the poetic and the vulgar that dream was! I think in bemusement. The early Zen priest Daie is said to have suffered greatly from the fact that even the enlightened mind, which has mastered the illusion of reality, is still troubled by dreams of the vulgar world. I can quite see his point. One whose calling in life is the arts surely doesn't cut much of a figure if his dreams aren't a bit more tasteful than the norm. I roll over, thinking to myself that most of my dream is quite useless from the point of view of a painting or a poem—and suddenly moonlight is pouring in through the paper screen doors onto the balcony, steeping them with the slanting shadows of several branches from the tree beyond. It is a brilliantly clear spring night.

Perhaps I am imagining it, but I think I can hear someone softly singing. I strain to catch the sound, wondering whether the song of my dream has somehow slipped out into the real world, or whether a voice from the real world has insinuated itself into the distant realm of my dream. Yes, someone is definitely singing. Small, low voice though it is, a thin thread of sound is pulsing faintly in the sleepy spring night. Strangely, it's not only the melody that comes to me; when I concentrate, I can also make out the song's words, though catching them from such distant singing would seem impossible. They are repeating over and over the song of the Nagara maiden:

> As the autumn's dew
> that lies a moment on the tips
> of the seeding grass,
> so do I know that I too must
> fade and be gone from this brief world.

At first the voice sounds quite close to the balcony, but it grows gradually fainter and more distant. When a thing finishes abruptly, you register the abruptness of its ending, and the loss is not deeply moving to you. A voice that breaks off decisively will produce a decisive feeling of completion in the listener. But when a phenomenon fades naturally away toward nothing with no real pause or break, the listening heart shrinks with each dwindling minute and each waning second to a thinner forlornness. Like the beloved dying husband who yet does not die, the guttering flame that still flickers on, this song racks my heart with anticipation of its end and holds within its melody all the bitter sorrows of the world's transient springs.

I have been listening from my bed, and as the song grows more distant, my ears ache to follow, though aware that they are being lured. With the dwindling of that voice, these ears long to rise of their own accord and fly in yearning pursuit of it. A bare second before the last pulse of sound must surely no longer reach my straining hearing, I can bear it no longer, and in a moment I have slipped from the bed and opened the screen doors to the balcony. The lower part of my legs is instantly bathed in moonlight. The tree shadows fall wavering over my night robe.

When I first slide open the paper doors, I notice none of this. Where is that voice? My eyes seek the place where my eager ears have already guessed the answer lies—and there it stands, a vague shadowy shape withdrawn from the moonlight, its back to the trunk of what, judging from the blossoms, might be an aronia tree. Before I have even an instant to try to comprehend what it is, the black shape turns and moves off to the right, trampling the shadow of the blossoms as it goes. Then a tall woman's form slides fluidly around the corner, and the edge of the building that my own room is part of hides her instantly from sight.

I stand entranced at the doors awhile longer, clad only in the single layer of the inn's night robe, until I come to myself again and realize that the spring night in this mountain village is in fact extremely cold. Then I return to the hollow of bedclothes from which I earlier emerged, where I begin to ponder what I have just witnessed. I extract my pocket watch from beneath the pillow. It is ten minutes past one. Pushing it back under the pillow, I think some more. This can't possibly have been an apparition. If it wasn't an apparition, it must be a human, and if human, it was a woman. Perhaps it was the daughter of the

household. But it's surely rather unseemly for a woman separated from her husband to come out at night like this into a
garden, and one that merges into the wild hill beyond. Well, be
that as it may, the fact is I can't sleep. Even the watch under my
pillow intrudes on my thoughts with its ticking. I've never been
bothered before by the sound of my pocket watch, but tonight
it seems to be urging and berating me—*Let's think, let's think,*
it instructs. *Don't sleep, don't sleep.* Damn the thing!

If you see something frightening simply as what it is, there's
poetry in it; if you step back from your reactions and view
something uncanny on its own terms, simply as an uncanny
thing, there's a painting there. It's precisely the same if you
choose to take heartbreak as the subject for art. You must forget the pain of your own broken heart and simply visualize in
objective terms the tender moments, the moments of empathy
or unhappiness, even the moments most redolent with the pain
of heartbreak. These will then become the stuff of literature
and art. Some will manufacture an impossible heartbreak, put
themselves through its agonies, and crave its pleasures. The average man considers this to be sheer folly and madness. But
someone who willfully creates the lineaments of unhappiness
and chooses to dwell in this construction has, it must be said,
gained precisely the same vantage point as the artist who can
produce from his own being some supernatural landscape and
then proceed to delight in his self-created magical realm. In
this respect the many artists of the world are madder and
more foolish than the average man, at least insofar as they are
artists. (I say nothing of how they may be in their everyday
guise.) While we are on our journey, shod in our straw sandals
as of yore, we may do nothing but grumble about its hardships
from dawn to dusk, but when we come to tell the tale to others, we will never make a murmur of such complaints. No, we
will speak smugly of its fascinations and pleasures and even
proudly prattle on about all those things that annoyed us so
much at the time. We do so not from any intention to deceive
ourselves, or to lie to others. Rather, the contradiction arises
because on the journey we are our everyday selves, while

when we tell its tale we speak as poets. I suppose you could say that the artist is one who lives in a three-cornered world, in which the corner that the average person would call "common sense" has been sheared off from the ordinary four-square world that the normal inhabit.

For this reason, be it in nature or in human affairs, the artist will see the glitter of priceless jewels of art in places where the common herd fears to tread. The vulgar mind terms it "romanticizing," but it is no such thing. In fact, the phenomenal world has always contained that scintillating radiance that artists find there. It's just that eyes blinded by worldly passions cannot see the true nature of reality. Inextricable entanglements bind us to the common world; we are beset by obsessions with everyday success and failure and by ardent hopes—and so we pass by unheeding, until a Turner reveals for us in his painting the splendor of the steam train, or an Ōkyo gives us the beauty of a ghost.[5]

The apparition I have just seen, if viewed simply as that, would certainly be rich with poetry for anyone, no matter who saw or spoke of it. A hot spring in some little village tucked away from the world, the shadow of blossoms on a spring evening, murmured song in moonlight, a dimly lit figure—every element is a perfect subject for the artist. And here I am, confronted with this perfect subject, engaging in useless debates and inquiries on it! Chill reason has intruded itself on this precious realm of refined beauty; tremulous distaste has trampled upon this unsought moment of artistic elegance. Under the circumstances, it's meaningless to profess my vaunted "nonemotional" approach. I must put myself through a bit more training in the discipline before I'm qualified to boast to others that I am a poet or artist. I've heard that an Italian artist of times gone by, one Salvator Rosa, risked his life to join a gang of bandits through his single-minded desire to make a study of a robber.[6] Having so jauntily set off on this journey, sketchbook tucked into my kimono, I would be ashamed to show any less resolve.

In order to regain the poetic point of view on this occasion,

I have only to set up before myself my own feelings, then take a step back from them and calmly, dispassionately investigate their true nature. The poet has an obligation to dissect his own corpse and reveal the symptoms of its illness to the world. There are various ways to achieve this, but the most successful immediate one is to try jotting everything down in seventeen-syllable haiku form, with whatever words spring to mind. The haiku is the simplest and handiest form of poetry; you can compose one with ease while you're washing your face, or on the toilet, or on a train. But that's no reason to disparage the haiku. No one should try to claim that because the haiku is easily achieved, becoming a poet therefore costs one little, and since to be a poet is to be in some sense enlightened, enlightenment must therefore be easily achieved. I believe that the simpler a thing is, the greater is its virtue, and thus the haiku should rather be revered.

Let's imagine something has made you a little angry. Then and there you put your anger into seventeen syllables. No sooner do you do so than your anger is transformed into that of another. You cannot be angry and write a haiku at the same time. Or say you weep a little. Put those tears into seventeen syllables and there you are, you are immediately happy. Making a haiku of your tears frees you from their bitterness; now you are simply happy to be a man who is capable of weeping.

This has long been my conviction. Now the time has come to put my belief into action, and I lie here in bed trying out this and that haiku in my head. Since I must approach this task as a conscientious discipline, I open my sketchbook and lay it by the pillow, knowing that I must write down any poems that come or my focus will blur and my attempts come to nothing.

I first write

> The maddened woman
> setting the dewdrops trembling
> on the aronia.

Reading it over, I feel it isn't particularly interesting, but neither is it downright bad. Then I try

> Shadow of blossoms
> shadowed form of a woman
> hazy on the ground.

This one has too many season words.[7] Still, what does it matter? The point of the exercise is simply to become calm and detached.

> Inari's fox god
> has changed to a woman's shape
> under the hazed moon.[8]

But this one is quite absurd, and I have to laugh.

At this rate all will be well. I am now enjoying myself, and I begin jotting down poem after poem as each occurs to me.

> Shaking down the stars
> out of the spring night, she wears
> them bright in her hair.

> New-washed hair, perhaps
> dampened by moisture from the clouds
> of this night of spring.

> O spring! This evening
> that beauteous figure deigned
> to sing the world her song.

> Such a moonlit night
> when from the aronia tree
> its spirit issues forth.

> Poem upon poem
> wandering here and there
> in the spring moonlight.

Now at last the spring
draws swiftly to its finish.
How alone I am.

As I scribble away, a drowsiness creeps upon me.

Perhaps the word "entranced" is the most fitting to use here. No one can remain aware in deep sleep; when the mind is conscious and clear, on the other hand, no one can be completely oblivious to the outside world. But between these two states exists a fragile realm of phantasms and visions, too vague to be called waking, too alert to be termed sleep. It is as if the two worlds of sleep and waking were placed in a single pot and thoroughly mixed together with the brush of poetry. Nature's real colors are spread thin to the very door of dream; the universe is drawn unaltered a little way inside that other misty realm. The magic hand of Morpheus smoothes from the real world's surfaces all their sharp angles, while within this softened realm a tiny pulse of self still faintly beats. Like smoke that clings to the ground and cannot rise, your soul cannot quite bring itself to leave behind its physical shell. The spirit hovers, hesitant yet urging to find release, until finally you can no longer sustain it in this unfeeling realm, and now the invisible distillations of the universe pervade and wreathe themselves whole about the body, producing a sensation of clinging, of yearning love.

I am wandering in this realm between sleep and waking, when the door from the corridor slides smoothly open, and suddenly in the doorway appears, like a phantom, the shape of a woman. I am not surprised, nor am I afraid. I simply gaze at it with pleasure. The word "gaze" is perhaps a little strong. Rather say that the phantom slips easily in under my closed eyelids. It comes gliding into the room, traveling soundlessly over the matting like a spirit lady walking on water. Since I'm watching from beneath closed eyelids, I cannot be sure, but she seems pale, long-necked, and possessed of a luxuriance of hair. The effect is rather like the blurred photographs that people produce these days, held up to view against lamplight.

The phantom pauses before the cupboard. It opens, and a white arm emerges smoothly from the sleeve, glimmering softly in the darkness. The cupboard closes again. The waters of the matting float the phantom back across them to the door. The sliding door closes of its own accord. Gradually I slip down into a rich, deep sleep, a state that I imagine must resemble that in which you have died to your human form but have not yet taken on the horse or ox form that is to be yours in your next life.

How long I lie there, hovering in that realm between human and animal form, I cannot tell. I awaken with the soft chuckle of a woman's laughter sounding at my ear. The curtain of night has long since been drawn back; the world that meets my eyes is flooded with light. As I lie there taking in the sight of the sweet spring sunlight pouring brilliantly in, shadowing the bamboo latticework in the round window by the alcove, I feel convinced that nothing eerie could lurk in this bright world. Mystery has crossed back over the river of the dead and retreated once more to the limbo realm beyond.

I take myself off to the bathhouse in my night robe and dreamily float there with my face barely above the water for five minutes or so, feeling inclined neither to wash nor to leave. Why did I find myself in such a strange state last night? How extraordinary that the world should tumble head over heels like that between day and night!

Drying myself is too much of an effort, so I leave it at that and go back to the dressing room still dripping. But when I slide open the bathhouse door from within, another shock greets me.

"Good morning. I hope you slept well." The words are almost simultaneous with my opening the door. I had no idea anyone was there, so this sudden greeting takes me completely by surprise, and before I can produce any response, the voice continues, "Here, put this on." The owner of the voice steps around behind me, and a soft kimono is slipped over my shoulders. At last I manage "Why, thank you . . . ," turning as I speak, and as I do so the woman takes two or three steps back.

The supreme effort that goes into describing the features of a hero or heroine has long been a determiner of a novel's worth. Were one to enumerate all the words, in every language of East and West from classical times until today, that writers have devoted to evaluating the qualities of beautiful women, the list may well rival in length the complete canon of the Buddhist sutras. How many words would it take, I wonder, if I were to select from among this truly dismaying assemblage of adjectives those that might best describe the woman now standing three paces away, twisting her body diagonally to look at me out of the corner of her eye, comfortably taking in my astonishment and bewilderment?

In my thirty-some years I have never until this moment seen such an expression as is on her face. The ideal of classical Greek sculpture, I understand, can be summed up in the phrase "poised containment," which seems to signify the energy of the human form held poised for action. The resonance of such a figure subtly inheres in that moment before the figure moves and changes into unguessable energies, swirling cloud or echoing thunder, which is surely why the significance of that form still reaches us across the centuries. All the dignity and solemnity to be found in the world lies hidden beneath this quality of poised containment. Once the figure moves, what is implicit becomes revealed, and revelation inevitably brings some resolution into one thing or another. Any resolution, of course, will always contain its own particular power, but once the movement has begun, matters will soon degenerate into mere sludge and squalor, and there will be no going back to the harmonious serenity of the original form. For this reason, whatever has motion is always finally vulgar. The fierce sculptures of the temple guardians that Unkei created, or the lively cartoon figures of Hokusai, both ultimately fail for this simple reason.[9] Should we depict motion or stillness?—this is the great problem that governs the fate of us artists. The majority of the words used down the centuries to describe beautiful women can surely also be placed in either one of these two great categories.

But when I look at the expression of the woman before me, I am at a loss to decide to which category it belongs. The mouth is still, a single line. The eyes, on the other hand, dart constantly about, as if intent on missing nothing. The face is the classic beauty's pale oval, a little plump at the chin, replete with a calm serenity, yet the cramped and narrow forehead has a somehow vulgar "Mount Fuji" widow's-peak hairline. The eyebrows tend inward, moreover, and the brow twitches with nervous irritability; but the nose has neither the sharpness of a frivolous nature nor the roundness of a dull one—it would be beautiful painted. All these various elements come pressing incoherently in upon my eyes, each one with its own idiosyncratic character. Who can wonder that I feel bewildered?

Imagine that a fault appears in the earth where once stillness has reigned, and the whole begins to move. Aware that movement is contrary to its original nature, it strives to return to its original immobility; yet once unbalanced, momentum compels it to continue its motion, so that now we see a form that from sheer despair chooses to flaunt the movement enforced on it. Were such a form to exist, it would serve precisely to describe the woman before me.

Thus, beneath the derision evident in her features, I sense the urge to reach out and cling. From within the superficial mockery glimmers a prudent wisdom. For all the bravado that suggests her wit and spirit would be more than a match for a hundred men, a tender compassion wells in its depths. Her expression simply has no consistency; in the appearance she presents, enlightenment and confusion dwell together, quarreling, beneath the one roof. The singular lack of any impression of unity in this woman's face is proof of an equivalent lack of unity in her heart, which is surely owing to a lack of unity in her world. It is the face of one compelled into misfortune, who is struggling to defeat that misfortune. Unquestionably she is an unhappy woman.

Bowing slightly, I repeat my thanks.

In reply, she laughs briefly. "Your room has been cleaned.

Go and see. I'll call on you later." No sooner has she spoken than she twists swiftly about and lightly runs off down the corridor. I watch her go. Her hair is up in the simple butterfly-wing *ichogaeshi* style, and below the sweep of hair a white neck is visible. It strikes me that the black satin weave of the obi at her waist would be only a facing.

CHAPTER 4

When I return, dazed, to my room, I see that it has indeed been beautifully cleaned. The previous night's events still rather disturb me, so I open the cupboard just to check. Inside stands a small chest, and from the top drawer a *yūzen*-dyed soft obi is half tumbled out, suggesting that someone has seized a piece of clothing in haste and quickly departed. The upper part of the obi is hidden from view beneath alluringly gaudy clothing. To one side is a small pile of books. Topmost are a volume of the Zen master Hakuin's sermons and the first volume of *The Tales of Ise*.[1]

That apparition of the previous night may well have been real.

Idly plumping myself down on a cushion, I discover that my sketchbook has been placed on the elegant imported-wood desk, carefully laid open with the pencil still tucked between its pages. I pick it up, wondering how those poems I feverishly jotted down in the night will read the next morning.

Beneath the poem

> The maddened woman
> setting the dewdrops trembling
> on the aronia.

someone has added

> The crow at dawn
> setting the dewdrops trembling
> on the aronia.

Because it is written in pencil, I can gain no clear sense of the writing style, but it looks too firm for a woman's hand and too soft for a man's. Here's another surprise!

Looking at the next poem,

> Shadow of blossoms
> shadowed form of a woman
> hazy on the ground.

I see that the person has added below it

> Shadow of blossoms
> shadowed form of a woman
> doubled and overlaid.

Beneath

> Inari's fox god
> has changed to a woman's shape
> under the hazed moon.

is written

> Young Yoshitsune
> has changed to a woman's shape
> under the hazed moon.[2]

I tilt my head in puzzlement as I read, at a loss to know whether the additions are intended as imitations, corrections, elegant poetic exchanges, foolishness, or mockery.

"Later," she said, so perhaps she is about to appear with my breakfast. Once she's here, I'll probably be able to make a little more sense of things. Happening to glance at my watch, I see it's past eleven. How well I slept! Given the lateness of the hour, I'd be better off making do with only lunch.

I slide the right-hand screen door open onto the balcony and look out, in search of echoes of last night's scene. The tree that I judged to be an aronia is indeed so, but the garden is smaller than I thought. Five or six stepping-stones are buried in a carpet of green moss; it would feel very nice to walk there barefoot. To the left is a cliff face, part of the mountain beyond, with a red pine slanting out over the garden from between rocks. Behind the aronia is a small clump of bushes, and beyond a stand of tall bamboo, its ninety feet of green drenched in sunlight. The scene to the right is cut off by the roofline of the building, but judging from the lay of the land, it must slope gently down toward the bathhouse.

Casting my eyes farther, I see that the mountain slopes down to a hill, which in turn sinks to an area of flat land about four hundred yards wide. This in turn dives below sea level, to emerge abruptly from the water about forty miles out, in the form of Mayajima, a small island that I guess to be less than fifteen miles in circumference. Such is the geography of the Nakoi area. The hot spring inn is tucked in against the mountainside, its garden half-embracing the cliff face. The building is a two-storied one, but here at the back, owing to the slope, it becomes a single floor. If I dangled my feet from this balcony, my heels would brush the moss. It makes perfect sense that the previous evening I thought the place to be strangely devised, as I clambered in perplexity up and down its steep staircases.

Now I open the window to the left. Before me is a wide rock, naturally hollowed out in the middle; the reflection of a wild cherry tree lies steeping in the still pool of water accumulated there from the recent spring rain. Two or three clumps of dwarf bamboo are elegantly positioned to soften the angle of the rock. Beyond stands a hedge of what looks like red-berried *kuko* bushes; the sound of occasional passing voices suggests that directly beyond the hedge lies the steep road that climbs from the beach to the hill. The gentle southward slope on the farther side of the road is planted with a grove of mandarin trees, and at the edge of the valley another large stand of bamboo shines white in the sun. I have never realized till now that bamboo leaves give off a silver light when seen from a distance. A pine-clad mountainside rises above the bamboo grove, with five or six stone steps leading up between the pines' red trunks, so clearly visible I feel I can reach out and touch them. There must be a temple there.

I next open the sliding door that leads off the corridor to my room and go out onto the porch beyond. The railing runs around four sides of an inner garden, and across it, in the direction from which I guess the sea would be visible, stands a second-floor room. From the railing, I can see that my own room is level with this second floor—a tasteful arrangement. Given that the bathing area is below ground level, I could be said to be ensconced in a room at the top of a three-tiered tower.

The building is a large one, but aside from the room opposite, and another that is level with my railing around to the right, almost every space that looks likely to be a guest room (I know nothing of the living area or kitchen) is closed up. There must be virtually no guests here apart from myself. The outer wooden shutters remain closed over the sealed rooms even during the day, but once opened, it seems they aren't closed again even at night. Perhaps the front door is not locked at night either. It's an ideal place for me to happen upon in my journey to savor artistic "nonemotion."

By now it's nearly twelve, but there is still no sign of my meal. I'm beginning to feel distinctly hungry, but I set about mentally identifying myself with the hermit poet in his words "vast empty mountains, no one to be seen," and manage to induce a state in which I feel not the least regret at having to skimp a little.[3] Drawing a picture feels like too much trouble just now, and as for coming up with a poem, my mind is already immersed in the poetic—to actually compose something would be merely a waste of breath. Nor do I have any inclination to undo the box of two or three books that I've brought along, tied to my tripod, and read. I feel perfect happiness simply lolling here on the balcony in the company of the shadow cast by the blossoms, my back toasting in the warm spring sunlight. To think would be to sink into error.

Movement seems perilous. I would cease even to breathe if I could. I want to live like this for a whole fortnight, motionless, like a plant rooted deep in the floor beneath me.

At last footsteps are heard coming along the corridor and climbing the stairs. Listening, I realize that two people are approaching. The footsteps stop before my room, then one person wordlessly retreats. The sliding door opens, and I guess it will be the woman I saw earlier that morning, but in fact it's the maid of the previous evening who enters. I register a touch of disappointment.

"I'm sorry this is so late." She sets down the tray table containing my lunch. There is no explanation for the lack of breakfast. The tray contains a plate with a grilled fish and a garnishment of greenery, and when I lift the lid of the bowl beside it, a red and white prawn is revealed nestling there in a bed of fresh fern shoots. I gaze into the bowl, savoring the colors.

"Don't you like it?" asks the maid.

"No, no, I'm just about to have it," I reply, but in fact it looks too beautiful to eat. I once read somewhere an anecdote about the artist Turner at a banquet, remarking to his neighbor as he gazed at the salad piled on the plate before him that this cool fresh color was the sort he himself used. I would love to show Turner the color of these fern shoots and prawn. Not a single Western food has a color that could be called beautiful—the only exceptions I can think of are salad and radishes. I'm in no position to speak of its nutritional value, but to the artist's eye it is a thoroughly uncivilized cuisine. On the other hand, artistically speaking, everything on a Japanese menu, from the soups to the hors d'oeuvres to the raw fish, is beautifully conceived. If you did no more than gaze at the banquet tray set before you at an elegant restaurant, without lifting a chopstick, and then go home again, the feast for the eyes would have been more than sufficient to make the visit worth your while.

"There's a young lady in the household, isn't there?" I inquire as I put down the bowl.

"Yes."

"Who is she?"

"She's the young mistress."

"Is there an older mistress here as well?"

"She died last year."

"What about the master?"

"Yes, he's here. She's his daughter."

"You mean the young lady?"

"Yes."

"Are there any other guests?"

"No one."

"I'm the only one?"

"Yes."

"How does the young mistress spend her days?"

"Well, she sews . . ."

"What else?"

"She plays the *shamisen*."

This is a surprise. Intrigued, I continue. "And what else?"

"She visits the temple," replies the maid.

This is also surprising. There's something peculiar in this visiting temples and playing the *shamisen*.

"She goes there to pray?"

"No, she visits the priest."

"Is the priest learning the *shamisen*, then?"

"No."

"Well, why does she go there?"

"She visits Mr. Daitetsu."

Ah yes, this must be the same Daitetsu who did the framed piece of calligraphy above my door. To judge from its content, he's clearly a Zen priest. That volume of Hakuin's sermons in the cupboard, then, must be her personal property.

"Who normally uses this room?"

"The young mistress is normally here."

"So she would have been here until I arrived last night?"

"Yes."

"I'm sorry I've turned her out. So what does she go to Mr. Daitetsu's place for?"

"I don't know."

"What else, then?"

"Sorry?"

"What else does she do?"

"Um, various things . . ."

"What sort of things?"

"I don't know."

The conversation comes to a halt. I finish my meal, and the maid withdraws the tray table.

When she slides open the door to leave, suddenly there beyond, on the second-floor balcony across the shrubs of the little inner garden, I see revealed the head of that same woman, under its *ichogaeshi* curves of hair. Her cheek rests elegantly upon a raised hand, and her gaze is directed downward like the enlightened figure of the "Willow Branch" Kannon bodhisattva.[4] In contrast to my earlier sight of her that morning, she now presents a deeply serene figure. Doubtless it's because her face is lowered and her eyes do not so much as quiver in my direction that her features are transformed in this way. It used to be said that "the eye is the finest thing in the human form,"[5] and certainly its incomparably vivid expressiveness will always shine through. Beneath the railing with its twisted patterning where she quietly leans, two butterflies flutter upward, now drawing together, now dancing apart.

Because my door has been opened suddenly, the woman swiftly raises her eyes from the butterflies toward my room. Her gaze pierces the air between us like a poisoned dart and falls upon my brow without a flicker of recognition or greeting. Before I can recover from my astonishment, the maid has once more clapped the door shut, leaving behind her the easygoing indifference of spring.

I settle down to sprawl on the mat once more. The following lines spring immediately to mind:

> Sadder than is the moon's lost light,
> Lost ere the kindling of dawn,
> To travelers journeying on,
> The shutting of thy fair face from my sight.[6]

Imagine that I have fallen in love with the figure I've just seen, and have determined to dedicate my life itself to achieving a meeting with her, only to be smitten at that very instant by such a parting glance as this, a glance that fills my being with astonished delight or anguish. In that state I would undoubtedly have written just such sentiments in just such a poem as this. I might even have added the next two lines:

> Might I look on thee in death,
> With bliss I would yield my breath.

Happily, I am by now well past any susceptibility to the triteness of love and heartache, and I couldn't become afflicted with such agonies even should I wish it. Yet these few lines are richly redolent with the poetry of the event that has just occurred. Though in fact no such painful longing binds me to the figure opposite, I find it amusing to project our relationship into the scene of this poem, and to apply the poem's sentiments to our present situation. A thin karmic thread winds between us, linking us through something the poem holds that is true to this moment. But a karmic bond that consists of such a very tenuous thread is scarcely, after all, a burdensome matter. Nor is it any ordinary thread—it is like some rainbow arching in the sky, a mist that trails over the plain, a spider's web glittering in the dew, a fragile thing that, though marvelously beautiful to the eye, must snap at the first touch. What if this thread were to swell before my eyes into the sturdy thickness of a rope? I wonder. But there's no danger of this. I am an artist. And she is far from the common run of woman.

The door suddenly slides open again. I roll over to see, and there stands my karmic companion, poised on the threshold, bearing a tray that holds a green celadon bowl.

"You're sleeping again, are you? I must have disturbed you last night. I do keep disturbing you, don't I?" and she laughs. She shows not the least sign of shyness or concealment, let alone embarrassment. She has simply seized the initiative.

48 NATSUME SŌSEKI

"Thank you for your help this morning," I say again. This is the third time I've responded with a brief polite formula, I realize, and furthermore it has consisted each time simply of the words "thank you."

I am about to rise, but she swiftly seats herself on the floor beside me.

"Oh, don't get up. We can talk as you lie there," she says airily. That's true enough, I think, and for the time being I content myself with rolling over onto my stomach and lying chin in hands, elbows propped on the matting.

"I thought you must be bored, so I've made you some tea."

"Thank you." There are those words again.

The plate of tea sweets contains some splendid slices of the firm bean jelly known as *yōkan*. *Yōkan* happens to be my very favorite tea sweet. Not that I particularly want to eat it, but that velvety, dense texture, with its semitranslucent glow, makes it a work of art by any standards. I especially enjoy the sight of *yōkan* that has a slightly blue-green sheen, like a mixture of gemstones and alabaster—and this bluish *yōkan* piled on the plate glistens as if it has just this moment been born from within the celadon, so that my hand almost twitches with the urge to reach out and stroke it. No Western sweet gives this degree of pleasure. The color of cream is quite soft, I grant you, but it's rather oppressive. Jelly looks at first sight like a jewel, but it trembles and lacks the weightiness of *yōkan*. And as for those tiered pagodas of white sugar and milk, they're simply execrable.

"Mmm, that looks splendid."

"Genbei has just brought it back from town. I imagine you'd be happy to eat something like this."

Genbei appears to have spent the night in town. I make no reply but simply continue to gaze at the *yōkan*. I have no interest in who has brought it or from where—I'm more than happy simply to be registering a beautiful thing as beautiful.

"This celadon plate has a very fine shape. A wonderful color too. It's scarcely inferior to the *yōkan*," I remark.

She titters, and a faint, contemptuous smirk plays for a

moment on her lips. She must have interpreted my words as intended to be clever. Considered thus, my remark does indeed deserve to be despised—it's exactly the kind of thing a stupid man will come out with in a misguided attempt to sound sophisticated.

"Is it Chinese?"

"What?" She isn't aware of the plate at all.

"It certainly looks like it to me," I say, lifting the plate to examine the inscription on its base.

"If you like this sort of thing, I can show you more."

"Yes, please do."

"My father loves antiques, so there are a lot of such things here. I'll tell him you're interested, and you can have tea together sometime so he can show you."

I shrink a little at the mention of tea. No one is more tediously pompous than a tea ceremony master, who will fancy himself the quintessence of elegant refinement. Your typical tea master is deeply conceited, not to mention affected and fastidious to a fault. He ostentatiously clings to the cramped little territory he's marked out for himself within the wide world of sensibility, savoring his bowl of foam and bubbles with a quite ridiculous reverence. If that abominably complex set of rules and regulations that makes up the tea ceremony contains any refinement, then a crack army corps must positively reek of elegant sophistication! All those "right about turn! quick march!" fellows must to a man be the equivalent of the great tea masters. The art of the tea ceremony is something that the common merchant and townsman, lacking any education in the finer matters of taste, dreamed up through their ignorance of how refinement really works, by mindlessly swallowing whole and in mechanical fashion the rules that were invented after Rikyū's day.[7] Their pitiful conviction that it constitutes the height of refinement only makes a mockery of true sensibility.

"When you say tea, you mean the ceremonial sort?"

"No, there's no ceremony about it at all. It's the kind of tea you don't have to drink if you don't want to."

"Well then, I'd be more than happy to have a cup while I'm there."

She titters again. "My father loves to have someone to show his collection to. . . ."

"Does that mean I have to praise his things?"

"He's an old man, so he'd be thrilled if you did."

"All right, I'll give them a bit of praise, then."

"Oh, come on, why not make it a discount and praise them lots?"

It's my turn to laugh. "By the way," I remark, "you don't use the language of a country girl, do you?"

"You mean, even though I have the character of one?"

"As to character, country people are better than city folk."

"Well then, I've got the upper hand there."

"But you must have spent time in Tokyo, surely?"

"Yes, and in Kyoto too. I'm a wanderer, so I've been all over the place."

"Which do you prefer, this village or Tokyo?"

"There's no difference."

"Doesn't life feel easier in a quiet place like this?"

"Easy, difficult—you can make it whatever you want, depending on your state of mind. There's no point in moving to the land of mosquitoes because you're sick of the land of fleas."

"You could go to a land of neither fleas nor mosquitoes."

"If you know such a place, go ahead and show me. Go on," she persists, leaning closer, "show me!"

"I'll show you if you want," I say, picking up my sketchbook, and I draw—not a picture, since it's done quite on impulse—just a hasty sketch of a woman on horseback looking at a mountain cherry tree. "Here," I say, thrusting it under her nose, "come inside this world. There are no fleas or mosquitoes here." Will she register surprise? Embarrassment? I watch her, certain that she won't be upset.

She evades the problem by dismissing it. "What a cramped little world it is!" she exclaims. "It has only length and breadth. You like this sort of two-dimensional world? A crab is what you are."

I burst out laughing. The bush warbler that has just begun to call by the eave breaks off his song at the sound and flies away to a farther branch. We both pause in our talk and listen intently for a while, but once interrupted that voice will not easily begin again.

"You met Genbei on the mountain yesterday, didn't you?"

"Yes."

"And did you visit the grave of the Nagara maiden on your way here?"

"I did."

"'As the autumn's dew that lies a moment on the tips of the seeding grass so do I know that I too must fade and be gone from this brief world,'" she recites swiftly, without any modulation to her voice. I can't guess what has prompted her.

"Yes, I heard that poem at the teahouse yesterday."

"The old lady told you, did she? She came as a servant to our house originally, you know, before I went off as a . . ." she begins, then casts me a quick glance to see how I'll react. I feign ignorance.

"It was while I was still young. Every time she came I'd tell her the story of the Nagara maiden. She could never remember the poem, but eventually she heard it so often that she did manage to memorize it all."

"Aha, so that's it. I must say I wondered how she came to know something so difficult. But it's a touching poem, isn't it?"

"Is it touching? I wouldn't compose a poem like that, myself. To begin with, how silly to go throwing yourself into a pool."

"Yes, I suppose it is, now that you mention it. What would you do?"

"There's no question what I'd do. The only thing to do is to have the two men as your paramours."

"Both of them?"

"Yes."

"You're amazing."

"There's nothing amazing about it. It's perfectly obvious."

"Yes, I see—in that case you wouldn't have to commit yourself to either the flea world or the mosquito world, would you?"

"One can get by in life without having to think like a crab, after all."

At this moment the half-forgotten bush warbler, its full energy restored, bursts out with a startlingly splendid high-pitched call. *Hooo-hoKEkyo!* Once revitalized, the lilting calls begin to flow forth again seemingly of their own accord. "Body flung upside down," as the famous haiku has it.[8] The base of its swelling throat atremble, its "small mouth" almost split open with the fullness of its song, as the bird calls again and again.

Hoo-hoKEkyoo! Hooo-hoKEkkyoo!

"Now that is real poetry," she says firmly.

CHAPTER 5

"Pardon my asking, but I'm guessing you're from Tokyo, are you, sir?"

"I look like a Tokyo man, do I?"

"Look like it? Why, a single glance . . . First off, I can tell just from hearin' you speak."

"Can you tell whereabouts in Tokyo?"

"Yees, well, Tokyo's awful big, ain't it. But I'd make a stab it's not the downtown part. Uptown Yamanote area, I'd say. Maybe Kōjimachi? No? Well then, Koishigawa? Well, it must be Ushigome or Yotsuya, then?"

"Not too far wrong, yes. You certainly know your Tokyo, don't you."

"You wouldn't know it to look at me, but I'm an old Tokyo-ite myself."

"So that's it. I could tell you had some style."

He chuckles. "Not a bit of it! Just look at me now, misery that I am. . . ."

"So how did you end up spending your days in a place like this?"

"No kidding, you've hit the nail on the head there, sir. End up here is exactly what I've done. Just couldn't make ends meet. . . ."

"Have you always been boss of a barbershop?"

"Not a boss, a worker. What's that? Where, you say? I worked in Matsunaga-chō in Kanda. Tiny filthy little place it is, Matsunaga-chō, not even room to swing a cat. The likes of you wouldna heard of it. You know Ryūkanbashi

Bridge? What? Don't know that either? Ryūkanbashi, fa-mous bridge."

"Hey, could you soap that up a bit more? It's hurting."

"Hurts ya, does it? I'm the fussy type, ya know, not happy till I can dig right in and get every hair on yer face, like this, shavin' against the grain, see? Not something your barber of today does, oh no, he just strokes, he does. You just put up with it a bit longer."

"I've been putting up with a lot for quite a while now. Come on, add a bit more hot water or soap, can't you?"

"Can't take it, huh? It didn't oughta be that painful. Yer whiskers have gotten too long, that's what the problem is."

Reluctantly, he lets go of the pinch of flesh he's been grip-ping on my cheek. Then he takes down a wafer of red soap from the shelf, dips it briefly in cold water, and without fur-ther ado quickly runs it all over my face. I'm not at all used to the experience of having raw soap rubbed over me like this; nor am I too impressed with the water he dips it in, which looks as if it's been sitting there who knows how long.

My rights as a barbershop customer compel me to face a mirror. For some time now, however, I must admit I have felt the urge to forgo this privilege. A mirror fulfills its allotted purpose only if it has a flat surface that reflects the human face without distortion. If you set up a mirror that fails to meet these requirements and force a man to face it, you are committing willful damage to his features quite as much as does the bad photographer. The destruction of a man's vanity is no doubt a valuable aid to the cultivation of character, but there's no need to show a man a face that does less than jus-tice to his own, then insult him by asserting that it is himself.

The mirror that I'm at present compelled to gaze into has been thus insulting me for some considerable time. If I turn to the right, my face is all nose, while the left profile splits my face from mouth to ear. When I raise my head, my features are squashed flat, with an effect reminiscent of looking face-on at a toad. If I lower my face a little, my forehead suddenly towers like some freakish faery child of the long-headed god

Fukurokuju.[1] So long as I sit before this mirror, I am forced to double as all manner of ghoulish monster. Of course there's no getting around the fact that my own face is far from a thing of beauty, but the glaring defects of this mirror—its poor color, and the mottled patches of light where the reflective backing has peeled off—surely make it a supremely ugly thing in its own right. Granted that only a fool will take to heart the abuses heaped on him by an obnoxious child, nevertheless no one enjoys spending any length of time in the presence of the insulting brat.

And it's not only the mirror; this barber is no ordinary barber, either. When I first peered into the shop, I found him sitting there cross-legged, looking mildly bored, drawing at his long-stemmed pipe and sending a constant stream of smoke over a toy flag set celebrating the Anglo-Japanese Alliance that hung on his wall.[2] But now that I'm inside and have entrusted my head to his ministrations, this benign impression has received a shock. He wrenches and mauls so mercilessly, as he scrapes away at the whiskers, that I'm almost at a loss to decide whether I still hold any right of possession to my own head or whether all such power has now officially passed to him. At this rate, even were my head nailed firmly to my shoulders, it wouldn't survive intact for long.

During the time he is wielding the razor, this man becomes not barber but barbarian, quite beyond the accepted rules of civilization. Even while the razor is merely going over my cheeks, it rasps and grates; when it sets to work by my ear, the artery in my temple leaps in panic; and as the fearsome blade flashes at my chin, it produces an extraordinary crunching sound, like ice being crushed underfoot. And this is a barber who fancies himself the most consummate in the land!

To top it off, he's drunk. An odd smell envelops me whenever he drawls his "sirs" at my ear, and from time to time my nostrils are assailed by a peculiar vapor. When and how his razor may slip, and where it will fly when it does so, only fate can decide. I'm in no position to be able to guess myself, having yielded my face to his ministrations—even he who wields

the blade has no clear idea of his razor's aim, heaven knows.
I've surrendered myself to him on a mutual understanding, so
I don't intend to complain about the odd nick I might receive,
but if matters suddenly took a nasty turn and I were to have
my windpipe sliced open, that would be quite another matter.

"Only a greenhorn'd shave this way with soap, but it can't
be helped, with your tough whiskers, sir," he remarks, tossing
the wet bit of soap unceremoniously back onto the shelf. The
soap, however, refuses to obey and instead slithers off and
tumbles to the ground.

"Haven't seen you around much, sir," he continues.
"Come here recently, did you?"

"Just a couple of days ago."

"That so? Where're you based?"

"I'm staying at Shioda's."

"A guest there, eh? That's what I thought. Matter of fact,
I'm here thanks to the old gentleman meself. See, he was
down the road from me when he was up in Tokyo, that's how
I got to know him. Good fellow. Knows a thing or two. His
lady wife died last year, and he spends all his time messin'
about with his collection of stuff these days. Got some fan-
tastic things, they say. They'd fetch a fine price if he sold
them, the story goes."

"There's a pretty daughter there too, isn't there?"

"You wanna watch out for her."

"Why so?"

"Why? Well, I shouldn't be tellin' tales, but she's back
from a failed marriage, she is."

"Is that so?"

"'That's so' to say the least of it! There weren't no cause for
her to come back home really. She left because the bank went
bust and they had to watch their pennies—no sense of duty. All
very well while the old gentleman's still on his pins, but when
worse comes to worst, well, it'll be a bad state of affairs."

"Will it then?"

"'Course it will. There's bad blood with the older brother
in the main house."

"There's a main house, is there?"

"Main house is up on the hill. Go take a look. Great view up there."

"Hey, a bit more soap there, please. It's hurting again."

"These whiskers of yours do a lot of hurtin', I must say. Too tough, that's their problem. You need to put the razor to these at least once every three days, sir. If you think my shavin' hurts, you won't stand a chance with any other barber."

"I'll do that. I could come along every day, if you like."

"You plannin' on spendin' that long here, are you? Watch out. Better not. No good will come of it. You let yourself get hooked by that good-for-nothing girl, there's no tellin' what will happen."

"Why's that?"

"That girl of yours looks good, but she's a loony."

"Why?"

"Why? Look, the whole village says she's crazy."

"There must be some mistake there, surely."

"No, no, there's more than proof enough. Look, best just drop the idea. Too risky."

"Don't you worry about me. So what proof is there?"

"It's a weird story. Here, settle down and have a smoke if you like, and I'll tell you. Wash your hair for you?"

"No, let's leave it at that."

"I'll just get rid of the dandruff, eh?"

Without further warning, the barber brings ten filthy claws down hard onto my skull and commences to scrape them fiercely back and forth. His nails thrust themselves between every hair on my head, to and fro, with the speed and ferocity of a giant's rake whirling about over a barren wasteland. I don't know how many thousands of hairs my head holds, but as his fingers go gouging about, each one of them seems to be being ripped from its roots, and the surface that remains feels as if it's hatched all over in raised welts. The ferocious energy of those fingers transmits itself down through the skull and rattles my very brains.

"How's that? Feels pretty good, eh?"

"You certainly have astonishing powers."

"Eh? A fine massage like that gives everyone a lift."

"I feel as if my head's about to fly off."

"Feeling limp and feeble, are we? It's all to do with the weather. Spring sure does make the old body go all floppy, doesn't it? Ah well, have a smoke. You'll be feeling bored, all alone there at Shioda's. Drop over for a chat. We old Tokyo-ites, we got lots in common the others wouldn't understand, eh? So that girl comes along and says hello to you, does she? No sense of right and wrong, that's the trouble with her."

"Weren't you just going to tell me something about her when suddenly dandruff was flying around and my head almost went with it?"

"True enough, true enough. Can't keep a story together in this silly head of mine. Right, so then that priest feller gets all funny for her . . ."

"What priest is that?"

"That useless underling of a fellow at Kankaiji temple."

"I haven't come across any priest in the story yet, underling or otherwise."

"That so? Sorry, I'm a bit hasty. Fine figure of a feller he was, sort of priest who'd be hot for the ladies, bit of you-know-what. Ends up he sends a letter—hey there, hang on a moment. Did he come after her? Nah, it was a letter right enough. And then—there was, um—gone'n gotten a bit muddled here. Ah, right, yes, that's it. Big surprise, right?"

"Who got surprised?"

"She did."

"She got a surprise when she received the letter?"

"Well, it'd be another matter if she was the modest sort who'd get surprised, wouldn't it. Dear me, no, not her, nothing'd surprise that one."

"So who got surprised, then?"

"The feller what came after her."

"But you said he didn't come after her."

"Right. Got it around my neck a bit, too impatient. Gets a letter."

"So it was the woman, then."

"No, no, the man."

"You mean the priest."

"Sure, the priest."

"So why was the priest surprised?"

"Why? Well, he's in the hall saying sutras with the abbot when suddenly in she rushes." The barber snickers. "She's a loony right enough."

"Did she do something?"

"'If you love me so much, let's make love right here in front of the Buddha,' says she, just like that, and she throws herself around Taian's neck."

"Good heavens."

"Really shook 'im up, it did. Goes and sends a letter to a loony, and now just look at the shame she's caused him. So that night away he creeps, and puts an end to 'imself."

"He died?"

"Must've. How could he live after a thing like that?"

"How bizarre."

"Darn right. Still, if the other party's a loony, you'd be pretty depressed if you'd put an end to yerself, so maybe he's still alive, who knows?"

"It's a fascinating story."

"Fascinating? Why, the whole village was laughin' fit to bust. But as for her, she's crazy of course, so she just went about calm as you please, didn't turn a hair. Well, a fine sensible gentleman like yerself, sir, there'd be no trouble of that sort, but bein' who she is, you'd only have to tease her a bit, say, and who knows what mightn't happen."

"Perhaps I'll tread a bit carefully, then," I say with a laugh.

A salty spring breeze wafts up from the warm shore, and the barbershop curtain over the door flaps drowsily. The reflection of a swallow flashes across the mirror as the slanting shape comes diving in beneath the curtain to its nest under the eaves. An old man of sixty or so is squatting under the eaves of the house across the road, quietly shucking shellfish. Each click of his knife against a shell sends another red sliver of flesh tumbling into the depths of the bamboo basket, followed by a sudden glitter as another empty shell flies across a shimmering band of light to land two feet or so away. Is it oysters, or surf clams, or perhaps razor clams, lying there in that high mound of empty shells? Here and there the midden has collapsed, and some of its shells have slipped down to lie on the floor of the sandy stream behind, carried out of the transient world to a burial in the realm of darkness. No sooner is a shell's burial completed than a fresh one is added to the pile beneath the willow. The old man works on, tossing shell after shell through the shimmering sunlight, never pausing to ponder their fate. His basket seems bottomless, his spring day an endless tranquil expanse of time.

The sandy stream runs beneath a little bridge a bare twelve feet or so long and bears its waters on toward the shore. Out there where its spring flow joins the shining spring sea, fathoms of fishing nets are looped up to dry in an uneven jumble of lengths. Perhaps it is these that impart to the soft breeze, blowing in through the nets to the village, a warm, pungent smell of fish. That sluggish silver visible beyond the nets, like a dull sword melted to a shimmering swim of molten metal, is the sea.

This scene is utterly at odds with the barber beside me. If his character were more forceful, able to hold its own in my mind against the brilliance of the scene that lies all about him, I would be overwhelmed by the wild incongruity between the two. Fortunately, however, the barber is not so strikingly impressive. However overflowing he is with the old Tokyoite's bravado, no matter how he might bluster and swagger, the man is no match for the vast and harmonious serenity of the circumambient air. This barber, who does his best to shatter the prevailing atmosphere with his display of self-satisfied garrulousness, has swiftly become no more than a tiny particle floating deep in the far reaches of the felicitous spring sunlight. A contradiction, after all, cannot arise where the relative strength, substance, or indeed spirit and body of the two elements are irreconcilable; it can be felt only when two things or people are on a similar level. If the discrepancy between them is too vast, all contradictory relationship may well finally evaporate and vanish, and the two instead come to play a single part in the great life force. For this reason the man of talent can act in the service of the great, the fool can be an assistant to the man of talent, and the ox and horse can support the fool. My barber is simply enacting a farce against the backdrop of the spring scene's infinity. Far from destroying the tranquillity of spring, he is in fact achingly augmenting the sensation of it. I find myself savoring my chance encounter with such a happy-go-lucky pantomime buffoon on this vernal day. This ebullient braggart, all puff and no substance, provides in fact the perfect touch to set off the day's deep serenity.

In this state of mind, it strikes me that my barber is a fine subject for a picture or a poem, so I remain squatting there companionably, chatting about this and that, long past the time I should have left. Then suddenly a little priest's shaved head slips in between the shop curtains.

"Excuse me, could you do me a shave?" he says, and in he comes. He's a very jolly-looking little priest, in a white cotton gown with a padded rope belt and a black priest's robe of coarse gauze draped over it.

"Ryōnen! How's it going? I'll bet the abbot told you off the other day for dawdling, huh?"

"Not a bit of it. He gave me a pat on the back."

"Pat on the back because you went off on an errand and managed to pull out a fish while you were at it, huh?"

"He said he was pleased I'd given myself such a good time; it goes to show I'm wiser than my years."

"No wonder yer head's all swelled up like that. Just look at those lumps. Dreadful business to shave such a badly behaved noggin. Well, I'll let you off this time. But you just mold it into better shape before you bring it here again."

"If I have to remold it to suit you, it's easier to take it to a better barber."

The barber laughs. "Head's shaped funny, but you sure got a quick tongue."

"As for you, your hands are hopeless at shaving, but they sure know how to lift a sake cup."

"Whaddya mean 'hopeless at shaving,' goddamn you!"

"I didn't say it, the abbot did. No need to lose your cool. Come on now, act your age."

"Hrrmph. No joke—isn't that right, mister?"

"What?"

"These priest types, they all live the easy life perched up there in their temples. No wonder their tongues get so quick off the mark. Even this young feller, he's forever shootin' his mouth off—oops, head to the side a bit—to the side, I said, dammit—I'll give ya a cut if ya don't do as yer told, got that? There'll be blood, I'm warnin' ya."

"Hey, that hurts! Don't be so rough!"

"This is nothin'. How ya goin' to be a priest if ya can't put up with a bit of pain, huh?"

"I'm already a priest."

"Yer not the real thing yet. Speakin' of which, why did that Taian die? Tell me."

"But Taian's not dead."

"Not dead? Fancy that. I was sure he died."

"He turned over a new leaf after all that happened, and he went off to Daibaiji temple up in Rikuzen, to throw himself into his practice. He'll have reached enlightenment by now, I should think. It's a fine thing."

"What's fine about it? Never heard of no Buddhist teaching that says it's fine to do a flit like he did. You just look out, ya hear me? Don't you go makin' a fool of yerself with a woman. Speakin' of women, that loony goes visiting the abbot, does she?"

"I haven't heard of any loony woman."

"Get it through that thick bald skull, come on. Does she go or doesn't she?"

"No loony goes to visit, but Shioda's daughter certainly does."

"The abbot can pray all he likes, there's no curin' that one. That ex-husband of hers has cursed her."

"She's a fine woman. The abbot has a lot of praise for her."

"Well, it beats me. Everything's topsy-turvy once you're up in that temple of yours. Whatever he says, a loony's a loony—right, that's yer head done. Off you go quick smart, and get yerself a scolding from the abbot."

"No, I'd rather take my time about it and get a pat on the back instead."

"Do as you like, you impudent twerp."

"Pah! You're a shit-ass!"

"What did you say?"

But the freshly shaved head has already ducked through the shop curtains and is out in the spring breeze.

CHAPTER 6

It is evening. I settle at the desk, all the doors opened wide.

Not only are there few people in this inn, but the building itself is relatively spacious, so that here in my room, separated as it is by winding corridors from the realm of human intercourse where those few dwell, not a sound comes to disturb my contemplations. And today all is quieter still. The master of the house, his daughter, and the male and female servants seem to have all departed and left me here alone—departed not to some ordinary place but to the land of mists perhaps, or to the realm of clouds. Or perhaps cloud and water have moved closer, so that their little boat drifts unawares upon a sea so calm that the hand is too languid to reach for the tiller, then floats off and away until the white sail seems to become one with water and cloud, until at last even the sail itself must scarcely know how it might differ from them—perhaps it is to this distant realm that they have all departed. Or perhaps they have suddenly disappeared into the depths of the spring, their mortal bodies now transformed to spirit mists there in the vast reaches between heaven and earth, too insubstantial to be visible any longer even to the microscope's powerful eye. Or they have become skylarks, singing all day the delights of the mustard blossom's gold, and now, as the light fades, soaring to where the evening's deep violet trails its hues. Or perhaps as gadflies they have lengthened the long day with their labors, failing at the last to sip from the last flower's center its sweet accumulated dew, and now they sleep a scented sleep, pillowed beneath some tumbled camellia blossom. Whatever may be the case, it certainly is quiet.

The spring breeze that wafts emptily through the vacant house comes neither to gratify those who welcome it nor to spite those who would bar it. No, it is the spirit of the impartial universe, which comes of its own whim, and of its own whim departs again. Were my heart, as I sit here, chin cupped in propped palm, as empty as the room around me, the spring breeze would surely blow unbidden clean through it as well.

Knowing that it is the earth that we tread, we learn to tread carefully, lest it be rent open. Realizing that it is the heavens that hang above us, we come to fear the echoing thunderbolt. The world demands that we battle with others for the sake of our own reputation, and so we undergo the sufferings bred of illusion. While we live in this world with its daily business, forced to walk the tightrope of profit and loss, true love is an empty thing, and the wealth before our eyes mere dust. The reputation we grasp at, the glory that we seize, is surely like the honey that the cunning bee will seem sweetly to brew only to leave his sting within it as he flies. What we call pleasure in fact contains all suffering, since it arises from attachment. Only thanks to the existence of the poet and the painter are we able to imbibe the essence of this dualistic world, to taste the purity of its very bones and marrow. The artist feasts on mists, he sips the dew, appraising this hue and assessing that, and he does not lament the moment of death. The delight of artists lies not in attachment to objects but in taking the object into the self, becoming one with it. Once he has become the object, no space can be found on this vast earth of ours where he might stand firmly as himself. He has cast off the dust of the sullied self and become a traveler clad in tattered robes, drinking down the infinities of pure mountain winds.

It's not because I wish to put on superior airs to browbeat those who are tainted with the marketplace that I thus strive to imagine this realm. My only intention is to tell the happy news of the salvation that lies there and to beckon those who have ears to hear. The fact of the matter is that the realms of poetry and art are already amply present in each one of us. Our years may pass unheeded until we find ourselves in groaning decrepitude, but when we turn to recollect our life and enumerate the vicissitudes of our history and experience, then surely we will be able to call up with delight some moment when we have forgotten our sullied selves, a moment that lingers still, just as even a rotting corpse will yet emit a faint glow. Anyone who cannot do so cannot call his life worth living.

Yet the joys of the poet do not lie simply in immersing oneself in some moment, and becoming one with some particular object. At times one may become the petal of a flower or a pair of butterflies, or again like Wordsworth one may let one's heart be tossed in the blessed breeze as a crowd of daffodils. But there are also times when the ineffable beauty around one, some presence one can scarcely grasp, mysteriously masters the heart. One person will speak of being brushed by the shimmering winds of heaven and earth. Another will say he hears in his soul the harmonies of nature's ethereal harp. Yet another may describe lingering in some incomprehensible and inexplicable realm without boundary or limit, or wandering in the misty far reaches of the world. People may describe it as they will. Into just such a state of mind have I fallen as I sit here at my desk, spellbound and with a vacant gaze.

Clearly I am thinking about nothing. I am most certainly looking at nothing. Since nothing is present to my consciousness to beguile me with its color and movement, I have not become one with anything. Yet I am in motion: motion neither within the world nor outside it—simply motion. Neither motion as flower, nor as bird, nor motion in relation to another human, just ecstatic motion.

If I were pressed to explain, I would want to say that my heart is moving with the spring. Or that some spirit—compounded of all the colors of spring, its breezes, its various elements, and its many voices, condensed, kneaded together into a magic potion that is then dissolved into an elixir in the realm of the immortals and condensed to a vapor in the warmth of Shangri-la's sunlight—such a spirit has slipped in, unbeknownst to me, through my pores and has saturated my heart. Normally some stimulant provokes a sense of oneness, and this is why the experience is enjoyable. But in this experience of mine I can't say what I've merged with, so it entirely lacks a specific stimulant. For this very reason, however, it produces a fathomless and inexpressible pleasure. I'm not speaking of some superficial and boisterous elation, waves tossed in the abstracted mind by a pummeling wind. No, rather my state is like a vast ocean that moves between one far continent and another above invisible depths of ocean floor. It lacks the vigor that this image suggests—but that is all to the good, for where great energy arises, a hidden fear of the time when that energy consumes itself and comes to an end is always present. In normal circumstances there is no such fear. And in my present, even more tenuous state, I am not only far removed from all such sorrow at the thought of a dwindling of sustaining energy, I am indeed quite freed from the everyday condition of man, in which the heart knows judgment of good and bad, right and wrong. I say that my state is "tenuous" only in the sense that it is ungraspable, not to suggest that it is unduly feeble. Poetic expressions such as "sated with tranquillity" or "sunk in a halcyon calm" perhaps most fully and finely express such a state of mind.

How might I go about expressing this state in terms of a picture? No ordinary picture could embody it, that's quite certain. What we express with the word "picture" amounts to no more than the scene before our eyes, human figures or landscape, translated either just as it appears or through the filtering of aesthetic vision onto the surface we work on. If a flower looks like a flower, if water looks like water, and if human figures behave in the picture like humans, people consider the work of the picture done. A greater artist, however, will impart his own feelings as he depicts the phenomena and bring them to vivid life on the canvas. Such an artist endeavors to imbue the object he perceives with his own particular inspiration, and he does not feel he has created a picture unless his vision of the phenomenal world leaps from the brush as he paints. He will not venture to call a work his own if he does not feel that he has seen a certain thing in a certain way, felt in a certain way about it, and expressed that way of seeing and feeling with all due respect to the masters of his art, drawing sustenance from the old legends while nevertheless creating a work that is both utterly true and thoroughly beautiful.

These two kinds of artist may differ in their objective and subjective approach and in their depth, yet before either one touches brush to paper, he will wait for a clear stimulus from the outside world. But the subject I wish to depict is not so clear. Though I use all my powers of sensation in order to find an equivalent for it in the outer world, no form, no color, indeed no light shade or dark, no firm or delicate line, suggests itself. What I feel does not originate from outside; or if it does, it does not arise from any single scene present to my eye—I can point to no clearly visible cause for it. All that exists is a feeling. How might I express this feeling in terms of a picture? Or rather, what physical form might I borrow to embody it in a way that would make sense to others? This is the question.

In an ordinary picture, it's sufficient to portray the object; feeling is not in question. In the second kind of picture, the object must be compatible with feeling. In the third, all that exists is the feeling, so one is forced to choose some objective phenomenon as its expressive correlative. Such an object, however, is difficult to discover and, once discovered, difficult to make coherent. And even when it is coherently conceived, it often manifests itself in a form radically different from anything found in the natural world. An ordinary person, therefore, would not perceive it as a picture. Indeed, the artist himself acknowledges that it is not a reproduction of some select part of the natural world; he deems it a success if the feeling evoked at the moment of inspiration in some way translates itself onto the canvas, imparting a certain life to the mood that lies outside the sensuous realm, which is the work's true subject. I don't know whether any master has ever completely succeeded in performing this difficult task. If

I were to name a few works that have approached success in this way, I could point to Wen Tong's bamboo, and the landscape painting of the Unkoku School. The scenes created by Taigadō and the human figures of Buson also come to mind.[1] As for Western artists, their eyes are mostly fixed on the external phenomenal world, and the vast majority have had no truck with the higher realms of noble refinement, so I have no idea how many may have been able to impart some spiritual resonance to their depiction of an object.

Unfortunately, the sort of grace and elegance that Sesshū and Buson strove to depict is very simple and rather monotonous.[2] I could never approach these masters for their power of brushstroke, but the feeling behind my intended picture is more complex, and therefore difficult to summon and express within the single frame of a picture. I shift position, from chin propped on hands to leaning on folded arms on the desk before me, but still nothing dawns. I must somehow find the hues, forms, and tones that will stir in me as I paint, the sudden recognition that cries *Ah, here it is! This is myself!* I must paint with the lightning bolt of instantaneous and joyous discovery of a mother who has journeyed through all the realms of the land in search of her vanished son, never forgetting him for an instant, sleeping or waking, and then one day suddenly chances upon him at a crossroads. This is no easy task. If I can achieve it, the opinion of others will matter nothing to me. They can scorn and reject it as a painting, and I will feel no resentment. If the combination of colors I produce represents even a part of my feeling, if the play of the lines expresses even a fraction of my inner state, if the arrangement of the whole conveys a little of this sense of beauty, I will be perfectly content if the thing I draw is a cow, or a horse, or no definable creature at all. I will be content— and yet I cannot do it. I lay the sketchbook on the desk and gaze at it, deep in thought, until my eyes seem to bore right through the page before me, but still no form occurs to me.

I put down my pencil and consider. The problem lies in attempting to express such an abstract conception in the form of a picture. People are not so very different from one another after all, and no doubt someone else among them all has felt the touch of this same imaginative state and tried to express it in eternal form through one means or another. If this is the case, what means might he have used?

As soon as I pose this question, the word "music" flashes before my inner eye. Yes, of course! Music is the voice of nature, born of this kind of moment, pressed into being by its necessity. Now I realize that one should listen to and study music; unfortunately, however, I myself am quite unacquainted with this field.

I next turn my attention to the third expressive domain, that of poetry. I recall the German writer Lessing saying something to the effect that events whose occurrence depends on the passage of time constitute the realm of poetry, and propounding the fundamentalist theory that poetry and painting are essentially different.[3] Seen from this viewpoint, the realm I am urgently attempting to present to the world seems likely never to find its expression in poetry. Time may certainly exist in the mental state that gives me my delight, but it contains no events that develop through time. My ecstasy is not produced by A's ending and being replaced by B, which in turn disappears for C to be born. My joy is of a thing held motionless inside the one profound moment, and the very absence of motion means that when I try to translate the experience into common language, the material I use ought not to be arranged to flow within time. As with a picture, the poem should be composed simply by arranging objects in space. But what scene ought I bring to the poem in order to depict this nebulous and insubstantial thing? Once I achieve that, the poem will succeed even if it doesn't fit with Lessing's theory. Talk of Homer and Virgil is irrelevant. If poetry is a suitable vehicle for expressing mood, that mood need not be portrayed through chronological events; as long as the simple spatial requirements of a picture are fulfilled, the language of the poem will be adequate to the expressive task.

But what does theory matter? I have largely forgotten the contents of Lessing's *Laocoön,* but if I were to look thoroughly into it, I imagine I'd only become confused. Since I have failed to produce a picture, I decide at any rate to try a poem, and pressing my pencil to the page of the sketchbook I rock myself to and fro, waiting for something to emerge. I continue in this way for some time, hoping somehow to be able to move the point of my pencil from where it rests on the page, but quite without success. The experience feels rather like suddenly forgetting the name of a friend, having it on the tip of your tongue but being unable to produce it. You know that if you give up trying, the elusive name is likely to sink forever beyond reach.

Imagine you set out to mix a gruel of arrowroot. At first your chopsticks merely churn the powder and feel no resistance from the liquid. If you persevere, however, the liquid slowly grows viscous, and your hand grows heavier as it stirs. Continuing to stir without pause, you finally reach the point where you can stir no longer, and in the end the arrowroot gruel in the pan will, of its own accord, positively rush to glue itself to your chopsticks. This is precisely the process of writing a poem.

At last my lost pencil begins to find its way on the page, in fits and starts, gathering impetus as it goes, and after twenty or thirty minutes I have produced these few lines.

> The spring is at its height,
> My sorrow burgeons with the grasses.
> Soundless, the flowers fall in the quiet garden.
> The lute lies neglected in the vacant room.
> In her web the spider sits unmoving.
> An ancient scrawl of smoke curls at the eaves.

When I read it over, I realize it is in fact a string of images that could easily become a picture. I might as well have made it a picture in the first place, I decide. Then I wonder why a poem was easier to create than a picture. Having reached this point in my poem, the rest seems likely to follow without too much effort, but now I feel the urge to write sentiments that are impossible to transpose into a picture. After much hesitation over the possible choices, I finally produce the following:

> Sitting silent in this quiet world
> I sense a faint light deep within me.
> The human world is thronged with busyness
> Yet how could one forget such peace?
> By chance I gain a day's serenity
> and learn how hectic is the life of man.
> Where might I place this deep expansive calm?
> It belongs only to the realms of eternal sky.

I read it through from the beginning. It is not without merit, but it seems rather too dry and dull to really convey the exalted state I've just been in. While I'm at it, I decide to try another poem. Gripping my pencil, my eyes stray unconsciously toward the doorway—and at this moment the door is slid open, and I catch a sudden glimpse of a beautiful shape beyond, slipping quickly across the three feet or so of open space. Good heavens!

By the time my eyes have fully turned to take this in, the door is open and the figure is disappearing. The movement is over almost before my eyes can catch it, and the shape passes and disappears in an instant. My gaze is now riveted on the doorway, all thoughts of poetry abandoned.

Within a minute the figure re-emerges across the way. Silent and serene, the woman walks along the second-floor balcony opposite me, clad magnificently in a long-sleeved formal kimono. The pencil falls from my hand. I stare across the twelve yards or so of courtyard garden, breath held, while the lone figure appears and disappears, parading gracefully to and fro at the balcony railing as the evening spring sky, already freighted with cloud, grows gradually heavier with the promise of rain.

The woman has said not a word, nor sent so much as a glance in my direction. She walks so softly that even the sound of her own silk hem trailing behind her would not reach her ears. She is too distant for me to distinguish the details of the dyed colors in the lower half of the kimono; all I can make out is the transition, where the kimono's basic color merges into the design below, a delicate shading reminiscent of the boundary between night and day, that boundary that she too treads.

I know not how many times this figure in her trailing kimono walks up and down the long balcony corridor nor how long she has performed this strange perambulation in her astonishing clothes. Nor have I the least idea what her intention might be. It's a weird feeling, to watch her endlessly repeating her ritual, coming and going, appearing and disappearing in the frame of my doorway, so decorously and so silently, for reasons beyond my ken. If her action is some lament for the passing spring, why should it take such an insouciant form? And why should this nonchalant pose choose to clad itself in such finery?

Is it perhaps gold brocade that makes the obi at her waist so startle the eye as this spectral shape, this hue of the dying spring, for an instant entrancingly brightens the doorway's dark depths? Moment by moment the gaudy brocade comes and goes, swallowed now into the blue depths of evening, into unpeopled remoteness, now returning hither through those far reaches of space. The sight is redolent of the twinkling stars of spring that sink at dawn into depths of violet sky.

At last the heavens are on the verge of opening to swallow this bright shape into the realm of darkness. There is something supernatural about the scene, the figure dressed in clothing appropriate to a vibrant life surrounded by golden screens and silver candelabras, "each instant of spring's evening worth a wealth of gold," willingly fading without fear or resistance from the visible world. As I gaze at her through the swiftly gathering darkness, she seems to linger serenely in one place, then tread with the one measured step, without haste, without bewilderment. If she indeed has no knowledge of the impending peril of the darkness, she is the height of innocence.

If she knows but does not feel it as a danger, she is uncanny. Loitering thus, so serene and poised, between the realms of being and nonbeing, her original dwelling must surely be that blackness, and this temporary phantom is now in the act of returning into the obscure darkness of its true home. The real nature of this figure is suggested by her kimono, whose bewildering pattern inexorably melts and disappears into inky black.

Another image: when a beautiful woman falls into lovely slumber and in the midst of this sleep draws her last breath in this world, we who watch by her pillow are stricken with grief. But if to the given pains of existence a thousand pains are added in dying, the woman herself, weary of pointless living, would feel with those who watch over her that relief from her suffering would be nothing but merciful. But how does a young child who dies easily in his sleep deserve his fate? A child drawn down to the realms of the dead in sleep has lived its precious life in a blind moment, with no preparation for death. If someone must be killed, let him first feel the absolute karmic inevitability of the fact, resign himself, and die with a prayer on his lips. If before your eyes is only the vivid fact of death, without the conditions that naturally lead to death, then you long not to chant the last rites over the dying but to cry out and summon back those feet that have already stepped halfway into the other world. Perhaps she who is slipping unaware from her mortal into her immortal sleep suffers by being called back like this, being dragged unwillingly by the chains of existence that she was in the act of severing. Be merciful, she may think, and do not call me, but let me quietly sleep. And yet we long to call.

When the woman appears once more beyond the doorway, I have just such an urge, to call her back and save her from the depths of unreality—but when her dreamlike form glides across the three-foot-wide space before my eyes, I find myself speechless. The next time, I decide, but then once more she slips past. Why can't I speak? I wonder, and as I wonder she passes again. She passes without the least show of awareness

that someone might be watching, or might be gripped by anxiety for her. She passes in seeming indifference to the likes of
me, neither burdened by my fears nor pitying me for them. As
I watch, summoning myself again and again to call, the
clouds at last began to spill the moisture they have so long
withheld, and soft threads of rain close their melancholy curtain about that distant form.

CHAPTER 7

It's cold. Towel in hand, I set off down to the bathhouse.

After disrobing in the little changing room, I descend the four steps that bring me into the large bathroom. There seems to be no dearth of local stone. The bathroom floor is paved with granite; in the middle a bathtub the size of a substantial tofu seller's vat has been sunk about four feet into the ground, and unlike a normal tub, it too is lined with stone. The place has a name as a hot spring, so presumably the water contains a variety of mineral elements, but it is perfectly clear and thus a pleasure to step into. Lying here in the tub, I even take an occasional experimental sip, but it has no particular taste or odor. The water is reputed to have medicinal qualities, but as I haven't bothered to ask, I have no idea what ailments it cures. I suffer from no particular illness, so it hasn't occurred to me to wonder what the water's practical value might be. The only thing that comes into my head as I lower myself into the tub are the lines from Po Chū-i's poem, "Softly the warm spring waters / bathed the white beauty's skin." Whenever I hear the words "hot spring," I taste again the deep pleasure that these lines evoke, and indeed it seems to me that no hot spring is of the least value unless it can produce in me precisely the sensation summed up in these lines. My sole requirement for a hot spring, you might say, is that it fulfill this ideal.

Once I am in the deep bath, the water comes up to my chest. I can't tell from whence it issues, but it is continually flowing gently out over the edge of the tub. The stone floor never has a moment to dry, and the warmth of it underfoot fills my heart with a tranquil happiness. Outside, rain is falling—at first gently enough merely to haze the night, delicately imparting a subtle moisture to the spring air, but slowly the drops from the eaves begin to fall more rapidly, with an audible *drip, drip*. A thick steam fills every corner of the bathhouse to the very ceiling, so dense that it must be seeking a way out through any gap or knothole, however small, in the wooden walls.

Chill autumn fog, a spring mist's serenely trailing fingers, and the blue smoke that rises as the evening meal is cooked— all deliver up to the heavens the transient form of our ephemeral self. Each touches us in its different way. But only when I am wrapped, naked, by these soft spring clouds of evening steam, as now, do I feel I could well be someone from a past age. The steam envelops me but not so densely that the visible world is lost to view; neither is it a mere thin, silken swath that, were it to be whipped away, would reveal me as a normal naked mortal of this world. My face is hidden within voluminous layers of veiling steam that swirl all about me, burying me deep within its warm rainbows. I have heard the expression "drunk on wine" but never "drunk on vapors." If such an expression existed, of course, it could not apply to mist and would be too heady to apply to haze. This phrase would seem truly applicable only to this fog of steam, with the necessary addition of the descriptive "spring evening."

I pillow the back of my head on the rim of the bathtub, relax every muscle, and let my weightless body float in the translucent water. My soul too drifts lightly, like a jellyfish. When I am in this state of mind, the world is an easy place to inhabit. You unbar the doors of common sense that lock up the mind, and fling open the heart's barriers of worldly attachment. What will be will be, I think, afloat here in the water, at one with the surrounding medium. No life knows less suffering than the life of that which flows, and being in the midst of flow, with the very soul afloat on its waters, is an even finer thing than being a follower of Christ himself. Seen in this light, even a drowned body becomes an essentially

elegant, aesthetic object. I think the poet Swinburne, in one of
his poems, wrote of the happiness felt by a drowned woman.
Looked at thus, Millais's painting of Ophelia, which has always somehow disturbed me, is in fact a work of considerable
beauty. I have long wondered why he chose such an unpleasant
scene, but now I see just why it works as a picture. There is
undoubtedly something inherently aesthetic about a figure
drifting or sunk, or half afloat and half sunk, lying at ease
upon the flow. If you add an abundance of herbs and flowers
along the banks, and depict the water and the face and clothes
of the floating figure in serene and harmonious colors, there
you have your picture. And there is such peace in the expression of that floating girl that it almost belongs to the realm of
myth or allegory. Of course, if she were depicted writhing in
a spasm of agony, it would quite destroy the spirit of the
work, but on the other hand an utterly unalluring and indif-
ferent expression would convey no trace of human feeling.
What kind of face would work? I wonder idly. Millais's
Ophelia may well be successful on its own terms, but I sus-
pect that his spirit and mine inhabit different realms. Millais
is Millais, I am me, and I feel the urge to try painting an elegant picture of a drowned corpse after my own fancy. But
conceiving of the face I want for it isn't such a simple thing.

    Still suspended in the water, I next try my hand at compos-
ing a eulogy to the drowned figure.

> Rain dampens
> And the frost chills.
> All is dark within the earth.
> But in spring waters there's no pain
> Afloat on waves . . .
> Sunk beneath waves . . .

    I am floating there aimlessly, intoning these lines softly to
myself, when from somewhere I hear the plucked notes of a
shamisen. Now, for a man who calls himself an artist, it's em-
barrassing to confess that I have almost no notion of matters

to do with the *shamisen;* my ears have scarcely ever registered the difference between one modal tuning and another. But listening idly to the sound of those distant strings makes me wonderfully happy, lying here in a hot bath in a remote mountain village, my very soul adrift in the spring water on a quiet vernal evening, with the rain adding to the delight of the occasion. From this distance I have no idea what piece is being sung or played, which too holds a certain charm. But judging from the relaxed timbre of the notes, it might be something from the repertoire of the great blind *Kamigata* performers, played on a thick-necked *shamisen.*

When I was a child, a sake shop by the name of Yorozuya stood outside our front gate. On quiet spring afternoons the daughter of the establishment, a girl called Okura, would always take up her *shamisen* and practice the old *nagauta* songs she was studying. Whenever Okura began to play, I would slip out into the garden to hear her. We owned a plot for growing tea, around forty square yards, in front of which, to the east of the guest room, stood a row of three pine trees. They were tall trees, about a foot in girth, and the interesting thing was that they were visually pleasing only as a group, not individually. The sight of them always made me happy as a child. Beneath the pines crouched a garden lantern of rusted black iron on a slab of some kind of red rock, grim and immovable, like an obstinate little old man. I used to love to gaze at it. Around this lantern the nameless grasses that had pushed up through the mossy earth tossed fancy-free in the world's fickle winds, casting their scent and taking their pleasure in their own sweet way. I discovered a place to squat among these grasses, a space just big enough for my knees to fit, and my habit at this time of year was to go and sit there, absolutely still. Each day I settled down beneath those pines, glaring back at the grim little lantern and sniffing the scent of the grasses, as I listened to Okura's distant *shamisen.*

Okura must by now be well into marriage, and her face across the sake shop counter would be that of a solid householder. Do she and her husband get along well? Do the

swallows still come back each year to those eaves, their busy
little beaks laden with mud? Since that time I have never been
able to separate in my imagination the sight of swallows and
the smell of sake. Are those three pines still there, forming their
elegant configuration? The iron lantern has certainly disinte-
grated by now. Do the spring grasses remember the boy who
used to squat among them? No, how would they now recognize someone who even then passed only mutely through their
lives? Nor, surely, do they retain any memory of the daily echo
of Okura's voice as she sang "The Hemp Robe of the Mountain Monk," accompanying herself on the *shamisen*.

Those plucked notes have spontaneously recalled for me a
vision of the nostalgic past, and I am transfixed, once again
the artless boy who inhabited that world of twenty years
ago—when suddenly the bathhouse door slides smoothly
open.

Someone's come in, I think, turning my eyes to the doorway as I float. My head is resting on the rim farthest from the
door, and the steps leading down to the bathtub are diagonally visible to me about twenty feet away. But my searching
eyes still cannot discern any figure there. I wait alertly, hearing only the sound of the raindrops along the eaves. The
notes of the *shamisen* have ceased without my noticing.

A long moment later a form appears at the top of the steps.
The large bathhouse is lit by a single small lamp hung from
the ceiling, so even if the air were free of steam, it would be
hard to make out anything clearly at this distance; now, with
the thick steam held down by the evening's fine rain and pre-
vented from escaping, I cannot discern the identity of the
standing figure. Unless it descends one step and its foot goes
to the second, and the full light of the lamp bathes it, ad-
dressing this figure as either man or woman is impossible.

The dark shape takes a step down. The stone seems velvet
soft; indeed, to judge by the sound alone, one could easily believe the shape hasn't moved at all. But now the outline swims
hazily into view. Being an artist, my senses are unusually
acute when it comes to the human frame. The moment the

ambiguous figure moves, I understand that the person in the bathroom with me is a woman.

Before I can decide, as I float there, whether to warn her of my presence, the woman has appeared in her fullness before me. As I see her there, deep within the warm brimming steam that the million soft particles of light have tinged a hazy pink, her black hair drifting about her like a cloud, and her body held poised and erect, all thoughts of politeness, decorum, and moral conduct flee my mind; I am gripped by the single fervent conviction that I have discovered the subject for a splendid painting.

I cannot speak for classical Greek sculpture, but certainly those nudes that contemporary French artists are so committed to painting give me clear evidence of a striving to depict the blatant splendor of the human flesh, as well as keen disappointment at the lack of any real grace and refinement in the depiction. At the time I merely registered the fact that these works are somehow vulgar, but I realize now that I have all this time been troubled by my failure to understand the reason for their lack of taste. If the flesh is clothed, the beauty of it is hidden; but unless it is hidden, it becomes vulgar. Today's artists of the nude do not limit their skills to depicting the vulgarity of the unhidden; they are not content simply to present the human form denuded of its clothes. They do their best to thrust the naked figure out into the world of the fully dressed. They forget that being dressed is the normal state of man, and they attempt to bestow complete authority on the naked form. In their eagerness to cry out to the viewer, "Look, here is a nude!" they push beyond all natural bounds. When technique reaches such extremes, people are likely to judge it as a vulgar coercion of the viewer. The attempt to make a beautiful thing appear yet more beautiful only detracts from its intrinsic beauty. "Riches breed loss," as the old saying about worldly affairs goes.

Reverie and innocence signify composure of mind, which is a necessary condition for painting, poetry, and indeed literature in general. The greatest evil in our present age of art is that the tide of civilization has swept artists along on its crest, goading them to an incessant state of pettiness and fussiness. The nude in art is a good example. The city has what are known as geisha, who trade in the art of flirtation and the erotic. In their dealings with the client, their only expressions are those calculated to make themselves appear as attractive as possible to him. Year after year the catalogs of our galleries are filled with nude beauties who resemble these geisha. Never for an instant do they forget their nakedness; indeed, their flesh squirms with the effort to display it to the viewer.

The graceful beauty before my eyes at this moment has about her not one jot of this crude worldliness. Normal people who divest themselves of their clothes thereby lower themselves to the baser realm of human existence, but she is as natural as a figure conjured from the cloudy realms of the age of the gods, innocent of any necessity for clothes and draperies.

The warm steam that is inundating the room continues to pour forth even though the room is already flooded with it to fullness. In the spring evening, the room's light is shattered and diffused into semitransparency, all asway in a world of dense rainbows, and from these cloudy depths, hazily, the pale figure gradually swims into view. Even the blackness of her hair is softened to the point of obscurity. Look at the contours of that shape!

A line begins lightly and modestly at the nape of the neck, then draws in from both sides to slide easily down and over the shoulders, breaks into ample curves that flow on down the arms till they no doubt finally part ways at the fingers. Beneath the full swelling breasts, the waves of line recede momentarily, to swell smoothly out again in the gentle curve of her abdomen. The line of force then slips around behind the form, and where the tension of the line gives out, the two columns of flesh tend slightly forward to balance it. The knees now receive the lines and reverse them, and when those long undulations have traveled to the heels, the flat plane of the feet brings all this intricacy to rest in effortless completion at the soles. The world could hold no more complex ten-

sion of forces, and none more unified. One could discover no
contours more natural, more soft and unresisting, less trou-
bling than these.

Moreover, this shape is not thrust blatantly before my eyes,
revealed like a common nude. The perfection of its beauty is
only modestly intimated, hinted in an ethereal atmosphere in
which all is transformed to profound subtlety. Like some apparition of a mythic dragon suggested to the imagination's
eye by a few brief flecks of scale within a brushstroke wash,
the shape is replete with a subtle air, a warmth, an unfath-
omable depth that satisfies every instinct of the artistic sensibility. If minutely depicting every scale on a dragon becomes
ludicrous, then equivalently, veiling a naked figure from full
and flagrant exposure to the eye resonates with a hidden pro-
fundity. Gazing upon this form, my eyes seem to be behold-
ing some faery moon maiden, fled from her lunar realm,
hesitating a moment before me as the pursuing rainbows
swarm about her.

The white form grows increasingly distinct. Another step,
and this delightful moon maiden may, alas, descend into the
common world—but just as the thought crosses my mind, her
jet-black hair swirls suddenly like the tail of the mythic turtle
that cleaves the waves, starting a sinuous undulation rippling
along its length, and up the stairs the white figure leaps, rend-
ing the swirling veils of steam as it goes. A woman's clear peal
of laughter echoes away down the corridor; in its wake, the
bathroom falls quiet.

I gulp in a mouthful of hot water and stand stock-still in
the bathtub, while startled waves lap at my chest, spilling
with a soft whoosh over the tub's edge.

CHAPTER 8

I take tea with the master of the house, Mr. Shioda. The other guests present are the abbot of Kankaiji temple, who introduces himself as Daitetsu, and a layman, a young man of twenty-four or -five.

Taking a right turn along the corridor from my door and then a left at the end has led me to the old gentleman's room, which is down at the far end. The room is a six-mat one, about twelve feet by nine, and a large, low sandalwood table occupies the center, imparting an unexpectedly cramped feeling to the space. Instead of the usual cushions surrounding it, there's a carpet with a woven flower design. It is no doubt Chinese. In its center is a hexagon containing a scene depicting a rather strange house and an odd willow. The surrounding ground is an almost steel-blue indigo, and at each corner is a brown circle, through which is woven an arabesque design. I doubt that such a thing would actually be found in a Chinese sitting room, but it is certainly most intriguing here, in place of the normal cushions. Just as the worth of an Indian cotton print or a Persian wall hanging lies in its slight oddness, so this flowered carpet's generosity and lack of fuss constitute its tastefulness. All such Chinese household furnishings, indeed, have the same rather dull and unimaginative quality. One is forced to the conclusion that they're the inventions of a race of patient and slightly slow-witted people. The special value of these objects is the way they daze and bemuse the viewer. Japan's works of art, on the other hand, are created with all a pickpocket's fine-tuned alertness. The West creates on a grand and detailed scale, which can never quite free itself of the reek of world-liness.

Such are the thoughts in my head as I take my seat. The young man places himself beside me, halfway down the length of the carpet.

The abbot is seated on a tiger skin, whose tail spreads past my knees while the head lies beneath the old gentleman. All the gentleman's hair seems to have been removed and transplanted onto his face, so that his cheeks and chin are smothered in a thick tangle of white beard. He is carefully arranging the teacups on their little saucers on the table before him.

"We have an unaccustomed guest staying, so I thought I'd take the opportunity of asking you to tea," he says, turning to the abbot.

"Thank you for sending someone along to invite me. I haven't gotten around to visiting for quite some time, and I was just thinking I must call in today." The abbot is close to sixty, with a round face and softened features reminiscent of one of those quick, freehand ink sketches of the Bodhidharma. He seems on familiar terms with the old gentleman. "This is your guest, I presume?"

The old gentleman nods as he lifts the little red clay teapot and lets the precious greenish-amber liquid trickle two or three drops at a time into the teacups. I am pleasantly aware of its elegant aroma gently invading my nostrils.

The abbot speaks to me immediately. "You must be feeling lonely here in the countryside by yourself."

"Er, well . . ." I say, unable to summon any real answer. If I say I'm lonely, it will be a lie, but if I say I'm not, a long explanation will be required.

"Not so, Your Reverence," our host chimes in. "This gentleman's come here to paint, so he's quite busy in fact."

"Ah, is that so? That's good. Would you be an artist in the Nansō School?"[1]

"No," I manage to reply this time. The abbot wouldn't understand it if I told him I painted in the Western style, I decide.

"No, he's in that Western style," the old gentleman says, coming to my aid once more in his role as host.

"Ah, Western, eh? That's the sort of thing Kyūichi does, isn't it? I saw his work for the first time the other day. Very nicely done, I thought."

"No no, they're just boring little things," the young man protests, breaking his silence.

"So you showed the abbot one of your poor pieces, did you?" the old man inquires. Judging from his attitude and the way he speaks to the young man, they're probably related.

"I didn't exactly request a viewing—he came across me when I was sketching at Mirror Pool," says Kyūichi.

"Hm, is that so? . . . Well now, the tea is poured. Do have some," the old man says, placing a cup before each of us. There are no more than three or four drops of tea in each, though the cups themselves are very large. The glaze is a light gray ground, daubed all over with burnt sienna and pale yellow brushstrokes that may have been intended as a painting or merely as a pattern, reminiscent of a half-formed devil's face.

"They're by Mokubei," he remarks simply.[2]

"They're delightful," I say, in equally simple praise.

"There are a lot of fake Mokubeis around. Look at the base. You'll find his signature there."

I lift it up and turn it toward the paper-screened window to see. The warm shadow of a potted aspidistra falls across the screen. Sure enough, when I twist my head to look closely at the base, I see the single small character "Moku." A signature is not really important in appreciating a work of art, but dilettantes apparently set great store by it. I bring the raised cup directly to my lips. A connoisseur with time on his hands will elegantly taste this rich, delicately sweet liquid, ripened in the precise temperature of the hot water, by letting it run one drop at a time onto the tip of the tongue. Most people believe that tea is to be drunk, but that is a mistake. If you drop it gently onto the tongue and let the pure liquid dissipate in your mouth, almost none of it remains for you to swallow.

Rather, the exquisite fragrance travels down to permeate the regions of the stomach. Using the teeth on solid food is vulgar, while mere water is insipid. The best green tea, on the other hand, surpasses fresh water in its delicate, rich warmth, yet lacks the firmness of more solid substances that tire the jaw. Tea is, in fact, a marvelous drink. To those who spurn it on the grounds of insomnia, I say that it's better to be deprived of sleep than of tea.

I next turn my attention to a blue stone tea-sweets dish that the old man has now produced and is passing around. It is nothing short of astonishing to consider the fine dexterity of the master craftsman who has carved such a large piece of stone to such thinness, and with such delicate precision! Spring sunlight shines through the translucent stone, seemingly captured and held there within its depths. It is right that such a plate remains empty.

"I brought this out to show our guest here. He's been kind enough to admire my celadon, so I thought I'd bring out a few more things for him to see today."

"What celadon would that be?" the abbot asks. "Oh, you mean the tea-sweets dish? I'm fond of that one myself, yes. By the way, I don't suppose Western pictures can be painted onto sliding doors, can they? If they can, then I'd like you to do me one."

Well, I think, I could do it if asked, but I don't know that it would be to the abbot's taste. There's no point in slaving to produce such a thing if he then declares that he doesn't like Western painting.

"I don't think Western painting would work for sliding doors," I say.

"You don't, eh? Yes, that's true, I suppose it would be a bit garish if it's the sort of thing I saw Kyūichi painting the other day."

"My paintings are terrible," protests the youth earnestly, looking most embarrassed. "I'm just messing around."

"Where is that pond you were speaking of?" I ask the young man, from idle curiosity.

"It's a lovely tranquil place, in the valley behind Kankaiji temple. It's just that I studied Western painting a little at school, you see, so I thought I'd stop by there and try my hand when I was feeling bored one day, that's all."

"And this Kankaiji temple . . . ?"

"That's where I am," the abbot breaks in. "A fine place. You can take in the whole sea at a glance from up there. Come and have a look while you're staying. It's only a half mile or so from here. From the corridor out there you can see the stone steps going up to it, have you noticed?"

"Could I come for a visit sometime?"

"Of course, of course. I'm always there. Mr. Shioda's daughter calls in quite a lot. Speaking of which," he says, turning to the old gentleman, "there's no sign of your Nami today. She's all right, I hope?"

"She must have gone out somewhere. Did she go to your place by any chance, Kyūichi?"

"No, she wasn't there."

"Probably off on a walk by herself again," says the abbot with a laugh. "She's got strong legs, has Nami. When I was out at Tonami the other day for a ceremony, I thought to my-self, 'Good heavens, that looks like Nami there on Sugatami Bridge,' and sure enough it was. She was wearing straw san-dals and had her skirts tucked up behind. 'What are you do-ing loitering around here, Your Reverence?' she says to me, quite out of the blue. 'Where are you off to?' Gave me quite a surprise, ha ha. 'Where in heaven's name have you been, dressed like that?' I ask. 'I'm just back from picking wild parsley,' says she. 'Here, I'll give you a bit.' And she suddenly shoves a muddy bunch of it into my sleeve, ha ha."

"Dear me . . ." says old Mr. Shioda, with a pained smile. Then he abruptly rises to his feet and turns the subject hastily back to curios. "I rather wanted to show you this."

He reverently takes down from the sandalwood bookcase a little bag made of fine old patterned damask. It seems to con-tain some heavy object.

"Have you ever seen this, Your Reverence?"

"What on earth is it?"

"An ink stone."

"That so? What sort of ink stone?"

"It was a favorite piece in Sanyō's collection."[3]

"No, I haven't seen that one."

"It has a spare lid done by Shunsui."

"No, haven't seen it. Show me, show me."

The old man tenderly undoes the bag, revealing a corner of the russet stone within.

"That's a lovely color. Tankei, would it be?"[4]

"Yes, and there are nine 'shrike spots.'"

"Nine?" repeats the abbot incredulously, evidently deeply impressed.

"This is the Shunsui lid," says Mr. Shioda, displaying a thin lid in a figured satin wrapping. A Chinese poem of seven characters is written on it in Shunsui's calligraphic hand.

"Ah, yes. He had a fine hand, a fine hand—though, mind you, Kyōhei wrote a better one."[5]

"You think so, do you?"

"I'd say Sanyō was the worst of them. That tendency to cleverness made him vulgar. Nothing interesting in him at all."

The old gentleman chuckles. "I know you're no fan of Sanyō, so I changed his scroll for a different one today."

"That so?" The abbot turns to look over his shoulder. The alcove is a simple recess in the wall. On its polished board stands an old Chinese copperware vase, its surface elegantly tarnished, with a two-foot-high branch of magnolia blossom arranged in it. The scroll hanging behind it is a large work by Sorai,[6] on a backing of subtly glowing figured silk. The calligraphy is on paper rather than the more usual silk, but the scroll's beauty lies not only in the indisputable skill of the writing itself but also in the delightful harmony between the backing and the paper, which has aged with the passage of time. The figured silk itself is not particularly wonderful, but it seems to me to achieve its fine quality through a combination of faded color and a softening of the effect of the gold thread, so that any original gaudiness has dimmed, allowing a certain austerity to assert itself. The two little ivory scroll ends protrude starkly white against the tea-brown background of the earth wall, while before the scroll softly floats the pale magnolia blossoms, yet the overall effect of the alcove is so calm as to be almost gloomy.

"Sorai, is it?" says the abbot, his head still turned to look.

"You mightn't care much for Sorai either, but I thought you'd prefer it to the Sanyō."

"Yes, Sorai's certainly far better. Calligraphers from this particular period always have a certain refinement, even if the writing's poor."

"Was it Sorai who said 'Kōtaku is a great Japanese calligrapher, while I'm just a poor imitator of the Chinese'?"[7]

"No idea. My own calligraphy certainly wouldn't be worthy of such a boast," says the abbot with a laugh.

"Speaking of which, Your Reverence, who did you learn from?"

"Me? We Zen priests don't read textbooks or do copying practice and suchlike, you know."

"Still, someone must have taught you."

"When I was young, I did study Kōsen's calligraphy for a while. That's all, though. But I'll do a piece anytime someone asks me." The abbot laughs again. "Now, could you let us have a look at that Tankei?"

At last the damask bag is removed. All eyes go to the ink stone that emerges. It's roughly twice as thick as a normal stone, about two and a half inches. The five-inch width and eight-and-a-half-inch length are fairly standard. The lid is polished pine bark that still retains its scaly texture, and on it in red lacquer are written two characters in an unknown hand.

"Now, this lid," the old gentleman begins, "this lid is no ordinary lid. As you can observe, there's no question that it's pine bark. Nevertheless . . ."

His eyes are on me as he speaks. As an artist, I'm unable to summon much admiration for a pine bark lid, no matter what its provenance and story, so I say, "A pine lid is a little inelegant, surely?"

The old gentleman holds up his hands in horrified remonstrance. "Well, if it's merely a common pine lid, I do agree, but this one—this one was made with Sanyō's own hands, from pine stripped from the tree in his very own garden while he was in Hiroshima."

Well then, I think to myself, Sanyō was a vulgar fellow, it seems. Rather daringly, I remark, "If he made it himself, he could get away with making it look a bit clumsier, I think. It seems to me he needn't have gone to the trouble of polishing up the rough patches to make them shine like that."

The abbot laughs heartily in instant agreement. "True enough," he says. "It's a cheap-looking lid." The young man turns his eyes pityingly to the old gentleman, who rather crossly takes the lid off and puts it aside. Now at last the ink stone itself is revealed.

If there is one thing particularly striking to the eye about this ink stone, it is the craftsman's carving on its surface. In the center a round area of stone about the size of a pocket watch has been left standing flush with the height of the edges, and it is carved into the shape of a spider's back. Eight legs go curving out in all directions, the foot of each consisting of one of the stone's characteristic "shrike spots." The ninth spot is visible in the center of the spider's back, a yellow stain like a trickle of juice. The remaining area around the spider's body and legs is carved back to a hollow about an inch deep. Surely this deep trench is not where the ink is intended to be ground? Two whole quarts of water would not fill it. I imagine one must dip a little silver ladle into an elegant water pot, trickle a drop onto the spider's back, and apply the ink stick there to create a precious pool of ink. Otherwise, though it is an ink stone in name, the object would be nothing more than a simple ornament for the desk.

"Just look at the texture of it, look at those spots!" The old gentleman almost drools with delight as he speaks.

Indeed, the color's beauty increases the more you gaze. If you breathed on that cold, lustrous surface, your warm breath might instantly freeze there, leaving a puff of cloudiness. The

most astonishing thing is the color of the shrike spots. They are
not so much spots as subtle shifts in color where the spot
emerges from the surrounding stone, a transition so gradual
that the eye finds it almost impossible to locate the point at
which the deceptive moment of change occurs. Metaphorically,
it's like gazing into a translucent plum-colored bean cake, at a
bean that lies embedded deep within. These shrike spots are so
precious that the presence even of one or two is highly prized.
There would be almost no examples of a stone with nine.
What's more, the nine are distributed equidistantly over the surface, so apparently systematically that the effect could well be
mistaken for a human artifact—a masterpiece of nature indeed.

"It's certainly a splendid thing," I say, passing it to the
young man beside me. "It's not just pleasing to the eye, it's
delightful to touch as well."

"Would you understand such matters, Kyūichi?" the old
man inquires with a smile.

"I've no idea," Kyūichi blurts out, ducking the question with
a rather desperate air. He puts the ink stone down in front of
him and gazes at it, then picks it up and hands it back to me,
perhaps acknowledging that it's too fine for his ignorant eyes.
I run my hands over it carefully one more time before returning it reverently to the abbot. He rests it delicately on the
palm of his hand till he's finished examining it; then, apparently not yet sated, he picks up the edge of his gray cotton
sleeve, rubs it fiercely over the spider's back, and gazes in admiration at the resultant luster.

"The color really is marvelous, isn't it? Have you ever used
this?" asks the abbot.

"No, I scarcely ever get the urge to actually use it. It's just
as I bought it."

"Yes, I can understand that. This would be considered rare
even over in China, I should think, wouldn't it?"

"Quite so."

"I'd like one of these myself, I must say," the abbot remarks. "Maybe I'll ask Kyūichi for one. How about it,
Kyūichi, could you buy me one?"

Kyūichi gives a chuckle. "I could well be dead before I get a chance to find you your ink stone."

"Yes, indeed. An ink stone will be the last thing you have on your mind, eh? Speaking of which, when do you set off?"

"I'm going in two or three days."

"See him off as far as Yoshida, won't you, Mr. Shioda?" says the abbot.

"Well, I'm an old man, and normally I wouldn't bother these days, but it may be the last time we meet, who knows, so I'm planning to go along and say farewell, in fact."

"There's no need to do that, Uncle."

So he's the old gentleman's nephew. Yes, I can see the resemblance between them now.

"Oh, go on," urges the abbot. "Do let him see you off. It would be quite simple if you went down the river by boat. Isn't that so, Mr. Shioda?"

"Yes, it's not easy over the mountains, but if we went around the long way by boat . . ."

The young man no longer objects to the offer; he simply remains silent.

"Are you going over to China?" I venture.

"Yes."

This monosyllable isn't an entirely satisfactory response, but there seems no need to delve further, so I hold my tongue. Glancing at the papered window, I register that the shadow of the aspidistra has shifted.

"Fact is," Mr. Shioda breaks in on his nephew's behalf, "with this war, you know . . . He enlisted as a volunteer, so he got called up to go." And so from him I learn the fate of this young man, who is destined to leave for the Manchurian front in a matter of days. I've been mistaken to assume that in this little village in the spring, so like a dream or a poem, life is a matter only of the singing birds, the falling blossoms, and the bubbling springs. The real world has crossed mountains and seas and is bearing down even on this isolated village, whose inhabitants have doubtless lived here in peace down the long stretch of years ever since they fled as defeated warriors from

the great clan wars of the twelfth century. Perhaps a millionth
part of the blood that will dye the wide Manchurian plains
will gush from this young man's arteries, or seethe forth at the
point of the long sword that hangs at his waist. Yet here this
young man sits, beside an artist for whom the sole value of human life lies in dreaming. If I listen carefully, I can even hear
the beating of his heart, so close are we. And perhaps even
now, within that beat reverberates the beating of the great tide
that is sweeping across the hundreds of miles of that far bat-
tlefield. Fate has for a brief and unexpected moment brought
us together in this room, but beyond that it speaks no more.

CHAPTER 9

"Are you studying?" she inquires. I've returned to my room and am reading one of the books I brought along, strapped to my tripod on the journey over the mountain.

"Do come in. I don't mind in the least."

She steps boldly in, with no hint of hesitation. A well-formed neck emerges above the kimono collar, vivid against its somber hue. This contrast first strikes my eye as she seats herself before me.

"Is that a Western book? It must be about something very difficult."

"Oh, hardly."

"Well, what's it about, then?"

"Yes, well, actually, I don't really understand it myself."

She laughs. "That's why you're studying, is it?"

"I'm not studying. All I've done is open it in front of me on the desk and start dipping into it."

"Is it interesting to read like that?"

"Yes, it is."

"Why?"

"Because with novels and suchlike, this is the most entertaining way to read."

"You're rather strange, aren't you?"

"Yes, I suppose I am a little."

"What's wrong with reading from the beginning?"

"If you say you have to start at the beginning, that means you have to read to the end."

"What a funny reason! Why shouldn't you read to the end?"

"Oh, there's nothing wrong with it, of course. I do it too, if I want to know about the story."

"What do you read if it isn't the story? Is there anything else to read?"

There speaks a woman, I think to myself. I decide to test her a little.

"Do you like novels?"

"Me?" she says abruptly. Then she adds rather evasively, "Yes, well . . ." Not very much, it seems.

"You're not clear whether you like them or not, then?"

"Whether I read a novel or not is neither here nor there to me." She gives the distinct impression that she takes no account of their existence.

"In that case, why should it matter whether you read it from the beginning, or from the end, or just dip into it in a desultory way? I don't see why you should consider my way of reading so strange."

"But you and I are different."

"In what way?" I ask, gazing into her eyes. This is the moment for the test, I think, but her gaze doesn't so much as falter.

She gives a quick laugh. "Don't you understand?"

"But you must have read quite a lot when you were young," I say, abandoning my single line of attack and attempting a rearguard action.

"I like to believe I'm still young, you know. Really, you are pathetic." My arrow has gone wide again. There's no relaxing in this game.

Finally pulling myself together, I manage to retort, "It shows you're already past your youth, to be able to say that in front of a man."

"Well, you're far from young yourself, to be able to make that remark. Is it still so fascinating, for a man of your age, all this talk of being head over heels and heels over head, and having pimples, and such adolescent stuff?"

"It is, yes, and it always will be."

"My, my! So that's how you come to be an artist, then."

"Absolutely. It's because I'm an artist that I don't need to read a novel from cover to cover. On the other hand, wherever I choose to dip in is interesting for me. Talking to you is interesting too. In fact, it's so interesting that I'd like to talk to you every day while I'm staying here. Come to think of it, I wouldn't mind falling in love with you. That would make it even more interesting. But we wouldn't need to marry, no matter how in love with you I was. A world where falling in love requires marrying is a world where novels require reading from beginning to end."

"That means that an artist is someone who falls in love un-emotionally."

"No, it's not *un*-emotional. My way of falling in love is *non*-emotional. The way I read novels is nonemotional too, which is why the story doesn't matter. I find it interesting just to open up the book at random, like this, like pulling one of those paper oracles out of the box at a shrine, see, and read whatever meets my eye."

"Yes, that does look like an interesting thing to do. Well then, tell me a little about the place you're reading now. I'd like to know what intriguing things emerge."

"It's not something one should talk about. Same with a painting—the worth of the thing disappears completely if you talk about it, doesn't it?"

She laughs. "Well then, read it to me."

"In English?"

"No, in Japanese."

"It's tough to have to read English in Japanese."

"What's the problem? It's a fine nonemotional thing to do, after all."

This could be fun, I decide, and proceed to do as she asks, falteringly translating aloud the words on the page. If there were ever a "nonemotional" way of reading, this is it, and she too, of course, will be hearing it with a "nonemotional" ear.

"'The woman emanated tenderness. It flowed from her voice, her eyes, her skin. Did she accept this man's help to lead her to the boat's stern in order that she might view Venice in the dusk, or was it to send this electricity coursing through his veins?' This is just a rough translation, you understand, because I'm reading nonemotionally. I may skip a bit here and there."[1]

"That's perfectly all right. I won't even mind if you add something wherever you feel inclined."

"'The woman leaned beside the man at the railing of the boat. The space between the two was narrower than that of a ribbon fluttering in the breeze. Together they bade farewell to Venice. The palace of the Doges glowed a soft red, like a second sunset, and faded from view.'"

"What's a Doge?"

"It doesn't matter what it is. It's the name of the people who used to rule Venice long ago. They ruled for generations; I'm not sure how many. Their palace still stands there."

"So who are this man and woman?"

"I've no more idea than you do. That's why it's interesting. It doesn't matter what relationship they've had till now. The interest lies in the scene before us at this moment, their being here together—just like you and me."

"You think so? They seem to be in a boat, don't they?"

"In a boat, on a hill, what does it matter? You just take it as it's written. Once you start asking why, it all turns into detective work."

She gives a laugh. "All right then, I won't ask."

"The usual novels are all invented by detectives. There's nothing nonemotional about them—they're utterly boring."

"Well then, let's hear the next bit of your nonemotional story. What happens now?"

"'Venice continued to sink from sight, until it became nothing more than a faint smudge of line against the sky. The line broke now into a series of points. Here and there, round pillars stood out against the opal sky. At last, the topmost belltower sank from sight. It is gone, said the woman. The heart of this woman bidding farewell to Venice was free as the wind. Yet the now hidden city still held her heart in a painful grip, and she knew she must return there. The man and the woman fixed their gaze on the dark bay. The stars multiplied above them. The gently rocking sea was flecked with foam. The man took the woman's hand, and it felt to him as if he held a singing bowstring.'"

"This doesn't sound very nonemotional."

"Oh no, you can hear it as nonemotional if you care to. But if you don't like it, we can skip a bit."

"No, I'm quite happy."

"I'm even happier than you are. Now where was I? Er . . . this part is somewhat trickier. I'm not sure I can . . . no, this is too difficult."

"Leave it out if it's hard to read."

"Yes, I won't bother too much. 'This one night, the woman said. One night? he cried. Heartless to speak of a single night. There must be many.'"

"Does the woman say this, or the man?"

"The man does. She doesn't want to go back to Venice, see, so he's comforting her. 'The man lay there on the midnight deck, his head pillowed on a coil of rigging rope; that moment in his memory, the instant like a single drop of hot blood when he had grasped her hand, now swayed in him like a vast wave. Gazing up into the black sky, he determined that come what may he must save her from the abyss of a forced marriage. With this decision, he closed his eyes.'"

"What about the woman?"

"'The woman seemed as one lost and oblivious to where she strayed. Like one stolen and borne up into thin air, only a strange infinity . . .' The rest is a bit difficult. I can't make sense of the phrasing. 'A strange infinity' . . . surely there's a verb here somewhere?"

"Why should you need a verb? That's enough on its own, isn't it?"

"Eh?"

There is a sudden deep rumble, and all the trees on the nearby mountain moan and rustle. Our eyes turn to each other instinctively, and at this moment the camellia in the little vase on the desk trembles. "An earthquake!" she cries softly, shifting from her knees and leaning forward against the desk where I sit. Our bodies brush each other as they shake. With a high-pitched clatter of wings, a pheasant bursts out of the thicket close by.

"Wasn't that a pheasant?" I say, looking out of the window.

"Where?" she inquires, leaning her pliant body against mine. Our faces are almost close enough to touch. The soft breath that emerges from her delicate nostrils brushes my mustache.

"Nonemotional, remember!" she says sternly as she swiftly straightens herself.

"Of course," I promptly reply.

In the aftermath of the little earthquake, the startled water in the hollow of the garden rock continues to sway gently to and fro; the shock has risen up through the water in a swelling wave that does not break the surface, creating instead a fine lacework pattern of tiny ripples in irregular curves. Were it to exist, the expression "tranquil motion" would describe this perfectly. The wild cherry tree that steeps its calm reflection there wavers in the rocking water, stretching and shrinking, curving and twisting; yet I am fascinated to observe that however its shape changes, it still preserves the unmistakable form of a cherry tree.

What an enchanting sight—so beautiful and shifting. This is how motion should be.

"If we humans could only move in that way, we could move all we liked, couldn't we?" she says.

"You have to be nonemotional to move like that, you know."

She gives a laugh. "You're certainly fond of this 'nonemotional,' aren't you!"

"I wouldn't say you were exactly averse to it either. That performance with the wedding kimono yesterday, for instance."

But here she suddenly breaks in coquettishly. "Give me a little reward!"

"What for?"

"You said you wanted to see me in my wedding kimono, didn't you? So I went out of my way to show you."

"I did?"

"I gather that the artist who came over the mountains put in a special request to the old lady up at the teahouse."

I can produce no appropriate response, and she goes on unhesitatingly, "What's the point of throwing my all into trying to please someone so hopelessly forgetful?" She speaks in a mocking, bitter tone. This is the second barb that has struck home, hitting me fair in the face, and the tide of battle is turning increasingly against me. She's somehow managed to rally, and now that she holds the upper hand, her armor seems to have become impregnable.

"So that scene in the bathhouse last night was purely kindness too, was it?" I try, scrambling to save myself from the perilous situation. She is silent.

"I do apologize," I go on, seizing the moment to advance when I can. "What should I give you as reward, then?" However, my sally has no effect. She is gazing with an innocent air at the piece of calligraphy by Daitetsu that hangs over the door.

After a pause she murmurs softly, "'Bamboo shadow sweeps the stair, but no dust moves.'" Then she turns back to me and, as if suddenly recollecting, studiedly raises her voice. "What was that you said?" I'm not going to be trapped again, however.

I try taking my cue from the tranquil motion of the water after the earthquake. "I met that abbot just a while ago, you know."

"The abbot from Kankaiji? He's fat, isn't he?"

"He asked me to do him a Western painting for his sliding door. These Zen priests say the most peculiar things, don't they?"

"That's how come he can get so fat."

"I also met someone else there, a young man."

"That would be Kyūichi."

"That's right, yes," I say.

"How much you know!"

"Hardly. I only know Kyūichi. I'm quite ignorant otherwise. He doesn't like talking, does he?"

"He's just being polite. He's still a child."

"A child? He's about the same age as you, surely."

She laughs. "You think so? He's my cousin, and he's off to the war, so he's come to take his leave of the family."

"He's staying here, is he?"

"No, he's in my older brother's house."

"So he came here specially to take tea, then."

"He likes plain hot water better than tea, actually. I do wish Father wouldn't invite people to tea like that, but he will do it. I bet his legs went numb from all that formal sitting. If I'd been there, I would have sent him home early."

"Where were you, in fact? The abbot was asking about it, guessing you must have gone off for a walk again."

"Yes, I walked down to Mirror Pool and back."

"I'd like to go there sometime. . . ."

"Please do."

"Is it a good place to paint?"

"It's a good place to drown yourself."

"I don't have any intention of doing that just yet."

"I may do it quite soon."

This joke is uncomfortably close to the bone for mere feminine banter, and I glance quickly at her face. She looks disconcertingly determined.

"Please paint a beautiful picture of me floating there—not lying there suffering, but drifting peacefully off to the other world."

"Eh?"

"Aha, that surprised you, didn't it! I've surprised you, I've surprised you!"

She rises smoothly to her feet. Three paces take her across to the door, where she turns and beams at me. I just sit there, lost in astonishment.

CHAPTER 10

I have come to take a look at Mirror Pool.

The path behind Kankaiji temple drops down out of the cedar forest into a valley, forking before it begins to climb the mountain beyond, and there, enclosed by the two ways, lies Mirror Pool. Dwarf bamboo crowds its edges. In some places the leaves press in so densely on either side that you can barely avoid setting up a rustling as you pass. The water is visible from among the trees, but unless you actually go around it, you have no way of guessing where the pool begins and ends. A walk around its perimeter reveals that it's surprisingly small, probably no more than three hundred fifty yards. However, the shape is highly irregular; large rocks jut out here and there into the water. What's more, the exact point of the shoreline is as difficult to judge as the pool's shape, for the lapping waves create a constant, irregular undulation along its edge.

The area around the pool is largely broadleaf woods, containing countless hundreds of trees, some not yet flush with spring leaf bud. Where the branches are relatively sparse there is even a carpet of young grass, sprouting in the warmth of the bright spring sunlight that filters through, and the tender forms of little wild violets peep out here and there.

Japanese violets seem asleep. No one would be tempted to describe them, as one Western poet has done, in the grandiose terms of "a divine conception" . . . but just as this thought crosses my mind, my feet come to a sudden halt. Now once your feet have stopped moving, you can find yourself standing in one place for an inordinate length of time—and lucky is the

man who can do so. If your feet suddenly halt on a Tokyo
street, you will very soon be killed by a passing tram, or
moved on by a policeman. Peaceful folk are treated like beg-
gars in the city, while fine wages are paid to detectives, who
are no better than petty criminals.

I lower my peaceful rump onto the cushion of grass. No
one will raise an objection even if I should choose simply to
stay sitting here for the next five or six days. That is the wonderful thing about the natural world; while on the one hand it
has neither pity nor remorse, on the other, it is neither fickle
nor arbitrary in its dealings with people—it treats all indiffer-
ently alike. Many are prepared to turn their noses up at the rich
and powerful, the Iwasakis and Mitsuis of this world.[1] But who
besides Nature can coolly turn his back on the ancient authority of emperors? The virtues of Nature far and away transcend
our pitiful human world; there absolute equality holds eternal
sway. Rather than associate with the vulgar and thus induce
in yourself the kind of misanthropic fury felt by Timon of
Athens,[2] far better to follow the way of the sages of old, to cultivate flowers and herbs in your little plot and spend your days
in peaceful coexistence with Nature. People like to speak loftily
of "fairness" and "disinterest." Well, if this means so much to
them, surely we would do best to kill a thousand petty criminals
a day and use their corpses to fertilize a world of gardens. . . .

But my thoughts have degenerated into mere tiresome
quibbles. I haven't come to Mirror Pool to engage in these
schoolboy ramblings! I take a cigarette from the packet of
Shikishima tucked in my sleeve and strike a match. Though
my hand registers the rasp, no flame is visible. I apply it to the
tip of the cigarette and draw, and only now, as smoke issues
from my nose, can I be certain I am smoking a lit cigarette. In
the short grass the discarded match sends up a little dragon
curl of smoke, then expires. I now shift my seat slowly down
to the shore. My grassy cushion slopes smoothly right on into
the pool; I pause just at the edge, where any farther advance
must bring the tepid water over my feet, and peer in.

The pool seems quite shallow for as far out as my gaze can

reach. Long, delicate stems of waterweed lie sunk there, in a deathly trance—I can think of no other way to put it. The grasses on the hill will bend with the breeze; stems of seaweed await the wave's tender, enticing touch. This sunken waterweed, immobile for a century and more, holds itself in constant readiness for motion; through the endless recurrence of days and nights, it waits, the tips of those long stems fraught with whole lifetimes of yearning, for that moment when it will find itself tousled at last into action. Yet in all this time it has never moved. Thus it lives on, unable still to die.

I stand and pick up from the grass two handy stones. I've decided to perform an act of charity for this waterweed. I toss one stone into the pool directly in front of me and watch as two large bubbles come gurgling up, to vanish in an instant. *Vanish in an instant, vanish in an instant,* my mind repeats. Gazing into the water, I can see three long stems of waterweed like strands of hair begin to sway languidly about, but in the next instant a swirl of muddy water wells up from the bottom to hide them from sight. I murmur a quick prayer.

The next stone I hurl with all my strength, right into the middle of the pool. There is a faint plop, but the tranquil pool refuses to be disturbed. At this, I lose the urge to throw any more stones; instead, I set off walking to the right, leaving my painting box and hat lying where they are.

The first few yards are an uphill climb. Large trees branch thickly overhead, and a sudden chill strikes me. A wild camellia bush is blooming in deep shade on the far bank. The green of camellia leaves seems to me altogether too dark, and there's no cheerfulness in them even when bathed in the midday sunshine or lit by a patch of sunlight. And this particular camellia is growing quite deep within a crevice in the rocks, huddled there in quiet seclusion, so that if it weren't for the flowers, one would never notice it. Those flowers! They are so many that a day's counting could not number them—though now that I've noticed those brilliant blooms, I feel almost tempted to try. Bright though they are, they have nothing sunny in them. They seize your attention like little sudden flares, but as you continue to gaze, you feel for some reason an uncanny shudder. No flower is more deceptive. Every time I see a wild camellia in flower, I think of witchery—a bewitching woman who draws people in with her black eyes, then quickly slips a smiling poison into their unsuspecting veins. By the time they realize the trap, it is too late.

When my eye falls on the camellia blooms on the far shore, I think to myself, Yes, better if you had not seen. The color of that flower is no mere red. In the far recesses of its dazzling gaudiness lies some inexpressible sunken darkness. The sight of a pear blossom sodden and despondent in the rain will provoke a simple pity; a coolly enchanting aronia blossom in moonlight calls forth only delighted affection. But the sunken darkness of the camellia is of a different order. It has a terrifying taste of blackness, of venom. And yet, with such darkness down there at its core, it decks out its surface in most flamboyant bright display. What's more, it does not set out to entice or even to attract the human eye. Flowers open and drop, drop and open, over the passage of how many hundred springs, while the camellia dwells on in tranquillity deep in the mountain shadow, unseen by mortal eyes. A single glance, and all is over! He who once lays eyes upon her will in no way escape this lady's bewitchment. No, the color of that flower is no mere red. It is like the red of a slaughtered criminal's blood, drawing the unwilling eye and filling the heart with unease.

As I watch, one of these red creatures plops onto the water. In all the quietness of that spring moment, only this flower has motion. A little while later another drops. These flowers never scatter their petals when they fall. They part from the branch whole and unbroken. The parting is so clean that they may strike us as admirably resolute and unclinging, yet there's something malignant in the sight of them lying whole where they have fallen. Another drops. If this continues, I think, the pool's water will grow red with them; indeed, the area surrounding these quietly floating flowers seems already tinged with crimson. There goes another. It floats there so still that one can scarcely guess whether it has landed on solid earth or on water. Another falls. Do they ever sink? I wonder. Perhaps the million camellia blooms that fall through the years lie steeped in water till the color leaches from them, till they rot, and finally disintegrate to mud on the bottom. Perhaps thousands of years hence and unbeknownst to men, all the fallen camellias will eventually fill this ancient pool till it reverts to the flat plain it once was. And now yet another tumbles to bloody the water, like a human soul in death. And another. A little shower of them plops to the water. Endlessly, they fall.

I wander back and have another cigarette, thinking idly as I puff that this might be a scene for my painting of the beautiful floating woman. Nami's joking words at the inn yesterday come snaking insidiously back into my memory. My heart rocks like a plank on a high sea. I will use that face, float it on the water beneath that camellia bush, and have the red flowers fall on it. I want to give a sense of the flowers falling eternally over the eternally floating woman—but can I achieve this in a picture? In Lessing's *Laocoön*—but no, who cares what Lessing said? It doesn't matter whether I choose to follow principles, what I'm after is the feeling. Still, remaining within the human realm, while seeking to express a sense of eternity that transcends the human, is no easy matter.

The face is the first problem. Even if I borrow her face, that expression of hers won't do. Suffering would dominate, and that would ruin everything. On the other hand, too great a sense of ease would also destroy the effect. Perhaps I should choose a different face altogether. I count off various possibilities, but none are suitable. Yes, Nami's face does seem to be the right one. Yet something about it isn't quite satisfactory. This much I know, but just where the problem lies is unclear to me, and consequently I can't simply change that face on some fanciful whim.

What would happen if I added a touch of jealousy to it? I wonder. No, jealousy has too much anxiety in it. What about hatred, then? No, too fierce. Rage? But that would wreck the harmony completely. Bitterness? No, too vulgar, unless it had a poetic air of romance to it. After pondering this and that possibility, I finally light on the answer: the one emotion that I've forgotten to include in my list is pity. Pity is an emotion unknown to the gods, yet of all the human emotions it is closest to them. In Nami's expression there is not one jot of pity. This is its great lack. When on an instant's impulse that emotion registers on her face, that will be the moment when my picture is complete. But when might I ever see this happen? The usual expression to be seen on that face is a hovering smile of derision and the intently furrowed brow of someone with a frantic desire to win. This is quite useless for my purpose.

A rustling crunch of approaching footsteps shatters my ideas for the painting well before they have arrived at a final form. Looking up, I see a man in tight-sleeved workman's clothing tramping along through the dwarf bamboo with a load of firewood on his back, making toward Kankaiji temple. He must have come down from the nearby mountain.

"Lovely weather," he says, taking off the little towel wrapped around his head and greeting me. As he bows, light flashes along the blade of the hatchet thrust into his belt. He's a strapping fellow, whom I guess to be in his forties. I feel I've seen him before somewhere, and he too behaves with the familiarity of an old acquaintance.

"You paint pictures too, do you, sir?" he asks. My painting box is open beside me.

"Yes, I came along hoping to paint the pool. It's a lonely sort of place, isn't it? No one passes this way."

"That's true. It's certainly deep in the hills here. But tell me, sir—you'd have had a good soaking coming over the pass after we met the other day, I should think."

"Eh? Ah yes, you're the packhorse driver I met, aren't you?"

"Yes. This is what I do, cut firewood like this and take it down to the town," says Genbei. He proceeds to lower his bundle to the ground and sit on it. A tobacco pouch comes out—an old one, whether paper or leather I can't tell. I offer him a match.

"So you cross that pass every day, eh? That's hard work."

"No, I'm quite used to it, really. And anyway, I don't go over every day. It's once every three days, sometimes even four."

"I wouldn't want to do it even once every four days, I must say."

He laughs. "Well, I'm sorry for the horse, so I try to keep it down to about every four days."

"That's good of you. So the horse is more important than you are, eh?" I remark with a laugh.

"Well, I wouldn't go that far. . . ."

"By the way, this pool strikes me as very old. How long can it have been here?"

"It's been here a long while."

"A long while? How long?"

"A very long while, believe me."

"A very long while? I see."

"I'll tell you this, it's been here since the Shioda girl threw herself in a long while ago."

"You mean the Shiodas who run the hot spring inn?"

"That's right, yes."

"You say the girl threw herself in? But she's alive and well, is she not?"

"No, not that girl. This one lived a long while ago."

"A long while ago? When would that have been?"

"Oh, a very long while ago, believe me."

"And why did that girl from a long while ago throw herself in here?"

"Well, she was a beauty, you know, like the present girl is, sir. . . ."

"Ah?"

"And one day, one of them bonzes came along . . ."

"You mean a begging monk?"

"Yes, one of them bonzes that plays the bamboo flute and goes about begging. Well, when he was staying over at Shioda's place—he was the village headman at the time—that beautiful young girl fell head over heels for him. Call it karma if you will, but at all events she wept and declared she simply had to marry him."

"Wept, did she? Hmm."

"But headman Shioda wouldn't hear of it. He said no bonze would be marrying his daughter. And in the end he cried, 'Be off with you!'"

"To the monk?"

"That's right. So then the young girl, she takes off after him and comes as far as the pool here—and throws herself in, right over there, where you can see that pine tree. And it all caused quite a stir, I can tell you. They say she was carrying a mirror on her, and that's how this pool got its name."

"Well, well, so someone's thrown themselves in here before, eh?"

"A dreadful business, sir."

"How many generations back would it be, do you think?"

"All I can say is it's a good long while ago. And I'll tell you another thing—well, this is just between you and me, sir."

"What's that?"

"There's been crazies in the Shiodas since generations back."

"Fancy that."

"It's a curse, that's what it is. And the present young lady too, everyone's been looking askance lately and muttering about how she's gone a bit peculiar."

"Surely that's not so!" I exclaim with a laugh.

"You think not? But her mom was a bit peculiar, you know."

"Is she at home there?"

"No, died last year."

"Hmm," I say, and make no further comment, but simply watch the thin curl of smoke rising from the end of my cigarette. Heaving the bundle of firewood onto his back again, Genbei goes on his way.

I've come here to paint, but at this rate, with my head full of such musings and my ear full of such talk, days will pass without me producing a single picture. Well, I've set everything up, so at least I must go through the motions and make a preliminary sketch or two. The scenery of the opposite shore will more or less do for what I want. I'll try my hand at it, just for form's sake.

A blue-black rock towers ten feet or more into the air, straight up from the bottom of the pool; to the right of its sheer face, where the dark water lies in a curve at the jutting corner, dwarf bamboo crowds densely all the way down the steep mountainside to the very water's edge. Above the rock a large pine tree at least three arm-spans thick thrusts its twisted, vine-clad trunk out at an angle that leans precariously half over the water. Perhaps it was from this rock that the girl leaped, the mirror tucked in her bosom.

I settle myself before the easel and survey the elements of the scene—pine, dwarf bamboo, rock, and water. I can't decide how much of the water to include. The rock and its shadow each measure about ten feet. One could almost believe that the luxuriance of dwarf bamboo extends beyond the water's edge on down into the water, so vividly does its reflection seem to penetrate right to the bottom. As for the pine, it appears to soar as high as the eye can see, while the reflection it casts is likewise extremely long and thin. Reproducing the actual dimensions of what lies before me wouldn't work as a composition. Perhaps it would be interesting to give up all thought of depicting the objects themselves and simply show their reflections. People would no doubt be startled to be shown a picture consisting only of water and the reflections in it. But it's pointless simply to surprise the viewer; what must surprise them is the realization that this is successful as a picture. What to do? I wonder, gazing intently at the surface of the water.

These weird shapes alone, however, simply don't resolve into a composition. Perhaps I could plan my composition around a comparison of the real objects with their reflections, so I let my gaze move slowly and smoothly upward, from the tip of the rock's reflection to the point where it meets the water's edge, then slowly on up; my eyes savor that glistening shape and climb attentively on over each curve and crevice. When finally they have completed their ascent and have arrived at the perilous summit, I freeze in astonishment, like a frog suddenly caught in the glaring sights of a snake. The brush falls from my hand.

There, vividly etched against the blue-black rock lit by the late spring sunlight, and framed from behind by the setting sun through green branches, is a woman's face—the same one that first startled me beneath falling blossoms, then as a ghostly form entering my room, then as a figure in flowing wedding robes, and yet again through the steam of the bathhouse.

My eyes are pinned there, unable to move from that pale face; she too remains perfectly motionless, stretched to her full supple height on the peak of the towering rock. What a moment it is!

Then without thinking, I spring to my feet. The woman twists swiftly about, and the next instant she is leaping away down the far side, with just a flash of what must be a red camellia tucked at her waist. The light from the setting sun brushes the treetops, softly tingeing the pine tree's trunk; the green of the dwarf bamboo intensifies.

She has astonished me yet again.

CHAPTER 11

I set off for a stroll, to savor the soft dusk of this mountain village. Climbing up the stone steps of Kankaiji temple, my mind produces the following lines for a poem in Chinese:

> Counting the stars of spring
> I gaze up—one, two, three . . .

I have no particular business with the abbot, nor any inclination to indulge in idle conversation with him. I've simply stepped out of the inn on impulse, letting my straying feet carry me where they will, and found myself at the base of these stairs. I pause here awhile, to run my hand over the stone pillar on which is carved the prohibition found at the entrance to every Zen monastery: "No alcohol or pungent vegetables permitted beyond this gate." But then a sudden flood of happiness sets me climbing the stairs.

In Sterne's novel *Tristram Shandy* the author claims that this book was written in the highest accordance with the will of God. The first sentence was created by himself, he says; the rest simply came to him, written while his thoughts were fixed on the Lord. He had no plan of what to write: though it was he who wrote the words, the words themselves were the Lord's, and therefore he holds no responsibility for them. Well, my stroll is of precisely this nature, though the irresponsibility is compounded in my case by the fact that I do not pray to God. Sterne managed very neatly to avoid responsibility by blaming it all on the Lord, while I, who have no God to take the blame on my behalf, simply cast mine into a passing ditch.

Nor do I exert myself in climbing the temple steps; indeed, if I found that the climb caused me any real effort, I would immediately give up. Pausing after I take the first step, I register a certain pleasure and so take a second. With the second step, the urge to compose a poem comes upon me. I stare in silent contemplation at my shadow, noting how strange it looks, blocked and cut short by the angle of the next stone riser, and this strangeness leads me to climb a further step. Here I look up at the sky. Tiny stars twinkle in its drowsy depths. There's a poem here, I think, and so to the next step—and in this manner I eventually reach the top.

Once I arrive I recall how, years ago, I visited Kamakura and spent some time calling on the big Zen temples there. I think it was at a subtemple in the Engakuji temple complex that I was plodding, just as now, up the long stone staircase that led to the temple gate, when a priest in saffron robes with a flat, bald head appeared above me. I climbed, and the priest descended. As he passed me, he demanded sharply, "Where are you going?" My feet paused as I responded simply, "To see the grounds." "There's nothing to see," he instantly shot back as he swept on. Somewhat disconcerted by his extreme curtness, I continued to stand there on the step, gazing at his receding figure, watching the flat head bob to and fro, to and fro, until he was lost among the cedar trees below. He never once turned to look back. Well, well, I thought, as I made my way through the temple gate, Zen monks are certainly intriguing. They have a fine brisk way about them. I looked around. There was no sign of life either in the main hall or in the spacious living quarters. Joy filled my heart at that moment. How deeply refreshing to know that someone so plainspoken existed, to be dealt with so wonderfully bluntly! My joy had nothing to do with any understanding of the truths of Zen Buddhist teaching; indeed, I had not the faintest idea of its meaning at that time. It sprang from the simple fact that this flat-headed priest delighted me.

The world is chock-full of unpleasant people—the pestering and spiteful, the pushy types, the fussers and nigglers. Some make you feel they're simply a waste of precious space on this earth. And it's always this sort who really throw their weight around. This fellow will consider the space he takes up to be a matter for tremendous pride. He feels his great purpose in life is to set a detective to work peering at your backside for years on end, counting your farts, and then he'll step out and stand there in front of you and make a song and dance about how many times you farted in the last five or ten years. If he says all this to your face, you can at least take note of what he's saying, but you'll find him insinuating things behind your back. Complaining just makes him more insistent. If you tell him to drop it, he nags all the harder. "Okay, I understand!" you cry, but, no, he just goes on and on about the number of farts. And this he claims to be his highest ambition in life. Well, everyone has their ambitions, and all I can say is, this fellow would do far better to drop his harping on about farts and fix on some goal that will shut him up. It's only common courtesy to put a hold on your ambition if it's going to cause problems for others. And if you say that your goal can't be fulfilled without bothering others, then I will say that mine requires me to fart—and there goes all hope for Japan.

To go strolling like this through a beautiful spring evening without the slightest goal in mind is the essence of cultured refinement. My sole aim is to let pleasure and amusement arise where they will—and if they don't, so be it. If a poem occurs to me, that poem will become my aim. If it doesn't, then that can be the aim. What's more, I am bothering no one; this must surely be the nature of a truly legitimate goal. That of fart counting is one of personal attack, while that of farting is justifiable self-defense. My present goal in climbing this flight of stairs to Kankaiji temple is to open myself, in the best Zen tradition, to the karmic moment.

When I reach the top, having gained the beginnings of a poem along the way, the faintly shimmering spring sea lies spread below me like an unrolled sash. I enter the temple gate. I've lost interest in finishing off my poem, so my new aim promptly becomes to abandon it.

The stone path that leads to the abbot's quarters is bor-
dered on the right by an azalea hedge, and beyond this probably lies the graveyard. To the left stands the main worship
hall. The top of its tiled roof glimmers faintly, and gazing up,
I have a sense that a million moons have cast themselves over
a million roof tiles there. From nearby there comes a pigeon's
insistent cooing—it seems they live somewhere under the
roof. I may be wrong, but the ground beneath the eaves appears to be scattered with small white dots—pigeon drop-
pings, perhaps.

Standing directly below the eaves' drip-line is a row of weird,
shadowy shapes. They're certainly not small plants of any sort;
nor do they look like trees. They make me think of those little
demons depicted praying to the Buddha in the painting of
Iwasa Matabei,[1] who have now left off their *nembutsu* prayer
and are waving their arms in the dance that accompanies it.[2]
They dance ceremoniously, forming a line that stretches from
one end of the worship hall to the other, while their shadows
dance ceremoniously in a line beside them, in exact replica.
The hazy moonlit spring night must have seduced them to
abandon the accustomed bell and book with which the *nembutsu* worshippers traveled the land, gathering together on
the moment's impulse to come to this little mountain temple
and dance.

When I approach, I realize they are in fact large cactuses,
seven or eight feet high. They look like green cucumbers the
size of gourds that have been crushed, molded into the shape
of flat spatulate rice paddles, and strung together vertically,
reaching skyward, their handles pointing down. How many
paddles would it take before their full height is reached? They
look as if they might this very night force their way up
through the eaves and climb to the tiled roof. Each new paddle shape, it seems to me, must appear quite suddenly, leaping
into place on the plant in the space of an instant; it seems in-
conceivable that an old one would bear a tiny new one, which
would grow slowly larger with the passing years. Those
strings of paddle shapes are utterly fantastical. How can such

an extraordinary plant exist? And so nonchalantly, what's more. When asked "What is the nature of the Bodhidharma's coming from the West?" a monk is said to have replied, "The oak tree in the courtyard"; if asked this question myself, I would reply without a moment's hesitation, "A cactus in the moonlight."

In my youth, I read a travel journal by one Chao Buzhi,[3] and I can still recite some of it:

It was in the ninth month—sky deep, dew pure and limpid, mountains empty, and the moon bright. When I looked up, all the stars were shining hugely, as if poised directly overhead. Outside the window a dozen bamboo stems, ceaselessly rustling as they brushed together. Beyond the bamboo, plum trees and palms crowded thick, like wild-haired witches. I and my companions looked at each other; we were all unnerved, and could not sleep. We departed as dawn was breaking.

Here I pause in my mumbled recitation and suddenly laugh. With a small adjustment in time and place, these cactuses might have unnerved me in just such a way and sent me fleeing down the mountain at the sight of them. I touch a spine with my finger and feel its irritable stab.

I turn left at the end of the paved path and arrive at the priests' quarters. Before it stands a large magnolia tree, whose trunk must be virtually an arm span in width. It stands taller than the roof of the building beside it. I look up into branches, and beyond them more branches, and there beyond this tangle is the moon. In another tree the sky would not be visible through such an interlacing, and the presence of flowers would obscure it still further; but between all these multi-layered branches is empty space. The magnolia doesn't try to confuse the eyes of the upward-gazing beholder with a jumble of twigs. Even its flowers are clearly visible; though I stare up from far below, each flower is a single, distinct form. I couldn't count how many of these single flowers throng the whole tree, in what state of bloom, yet each remains a separate entity apart, and between them the faint blue of the night sky is clearly visible. The flowers are not a pure white—such stark whiteness would be too cold. In absolute whiteness we can discern a ploy to arrest and dazzle the eyes of the viewer, but magnolia flowers are not of this order; these blooms modestly and self-deprecatingly avoid any extremity of whiteness with their warm creamy tinge. I stand awhile on the stone paving, lost in wonder, gazing up at this towering proliferation of tender flowers that plumb the very depths of heaven. My eyes hold nothing but blossoms. Not a leaf is to be seen.

The following haiku occurs to me:

> My eyes lift to see
> A sky that is entirely
> magnolia blooms.

Somewhere the pigeons are cooing softly together.

I step into the priests' quarters. The door has been left unlocked. This world seems to know no thieves; no dog has barked either.

"Anybody here?" I cry. Silence is the only reply.

"Excuse me?" I then try. The pigeons continue their soft *coo coo*.

I raise my voice and call again, and now from far away comes an answering cry: "Ye-e-e-e-s!" I have never before received this sort of response when I called at someone's house! Finally, footsteps are heard along the corridor, and a taper casts its light beyond the wooden partition. A small monk pops suddenly into view. It's Ryōnen.

"Is the abbot in?"

"He is. What brings you here?"

"Could you let him know that the painter from the hot spring inn is here?"

"The painter? Come on in."

"Are you sure you shouldn't ask him first?"

"No, it'll be fine."

I slip off my shoes and enter.

"You're not very well mannered, are you?" he says.

"Why?"

"You should put your shoes neatly together. Here, look at this." He points with his taper. Pasted onto the middle of the black pillar, about five feet above the earth floor of the entrance area, is a quartered piece of calligraphy paper on which some words are written.

"There. Read that. 'Look to your own feet,' it says, doesn't it?"

"I see," I say, and I bend down and arrange my shoes neatly.

The abbot's room is beyond a right-angle bend in the corridor, beside the main worship hall. At the entrance Ryōnen reverently slides open one of the paper doors and makes a low obeisance on his knees.

"Excuse me, but the painter from Shioda's is here," he announces, in a tone of deep deference that strikes me as rather funny.

"Is that so? Let him come in."

I replace Ryōnen at the entrance. The room is tiny. There's a sunken hearth in the middle, with an iron kettle singing quietly on the coals. The abbot is seated beyond it, a book in his hands.

"Come on in," he says, removing his glasses and laying the book aside.

"Ryōnen. Ryōooonen!"

"Ye-e-e-s!"

"A cushion for the guest, please."

"Ye-e-e-s!" Ryōnen's drawn-out cry floats back from somewhere in the distance.

"I'm glad you've come. You must be quite bored here."

"The moonlight was so lovely, I just wandered over."

"It's a fine moon," he says, opening the paper screens at the window.

Nothing is visible outside except two stepping-stones and a single pine tree. The flat garden ends at what appears to be a precipice, with the hazy moonlit sea directly below. Looking out produces the sensation of a sudden expansion of the spirit. The lights of fishing boats twinkle here and there out at sea, seeming at the far horizon to lift into the sky and imitate the stars.

"What a lovely view! It's a waste to keep the shutters closed, Your Reverence."

"That's true. But then, I see it every night."

"This view would still be lovely however many nights you saw it. If it were me, I'd stay up all night just to gaze."

The abbot laughs. "Of course you're an artist, so we're bound to be a bit different."

"You too are an artist, Your Reverence, when you find such a view beautiful."

"Yes, that's true enough, I suppose. Even I can do the odd Bodhidharma painting. Look at this one hanging here. This scroll painting was done by a predecessor. It's very good, isn't it?"

I look at the Bodhidharma painting on the scroll in the little alcove. As a painting, it's dreadful. All you can say for it is that it's not vulgarly ambitious. The painter has made not the slightest attempt to conceal its clumsiness. It is a naïve work. This predecessor must have been a similar type, someone who cared nothing for pretension.

"It's an unsophisticated painting, isn't it?"

"That's all our sort of painting requires. It only needs to reveal the painter's nature."

"It's better than the sort that's skillful but worldly."

The abbot laughs. "Well, well, that's a good enough compliment, I suppose. Now tell me, are there such things as doctors of painting these days?"

"No, there aren't."

"Ah, I see. Because I met a doctor the other day."

"Really?"

"I suppose a doctor is a fine thing to be, eh?"

"Yes, I imagine so."

"You'd think there'd be doctorates for painters too. I wonder why there aren't."

"In that case, there ought to be doctorates for abbots as well, oughtn't there?"

He laughs again. "Yes, well, maybe so. . . . Now what was his name, the fellow I met the other day? I must have his name card here somewhere."

"Where did you meet him? In Tokyo?"

"No, here. I haven't been to Tokyo for twenty years or more. I hear those things they call 'trains' are running these days. I wouldn't mind taking a ride on one to see what it's like."

"There's nothing very interesting about them. They're noisy things."

"Well, you know the saying—'The dogs in a misty country will bark at the sun, the cows in a hot country will pant at the moon.' I'm a country fellow, so I'd probably have a hard time coping with trains, in fact."

"Oh, I'm sure you'd cope perfectly well. They really are very boring things."

"Is that so?"

Steam is pouring from the iron kettle. The abbot takes a pot and cups from the nearby tea chest and proceeds to make us tea.

"Have a cup of coarse-leaf tea. It's not the delicious tea that Mr. Shioda makes, mind you."

"I'm sure it's perfectly fine."

"You look as if you wander about a lot. Now, is that in order to paint?"

"Yes. I take along the equipment when I go walking, but I don't mind if I don't actually paint any picture."

"Ah, so it's only half-serious, then?"

"Yes, you could say that. I hate submitting myself to all that fart counting, you see."

Even a Zen practitioner such as the abbot is apparently at a loss to comprehend this expression. "What do you mean by 'fart counting'?"

"If you live in Tokyo for a long time, you get your farts counted."

"How so?"

I laugh. "It wouldn't be so bad if it was just counting, but then they go on to analyze your farts, and measure your asshole to see if it's square or triangular, and so on."

"Ah, you're talking about hygiene, are you?"

"Not hygiene, no. I'm talking about detectives."

"Detectives? So it's the police, is it? Now, what's the purpose of policemen, eh? Do we really have to have them?"

"No, artists certainly have no need of them."

"Nor do I. I've never had any cause to bother one."

"I'm sure not."

"Still, I don't care if the police want to go counting farts. So what? They can't do a thing to you, after all, unless you've done something wrong."

"It's dreadful just to think something might be done to you on account of a simple fart, though."

"When I was a young monk, you know, my superiors always told me people never get anywhere with their training unless they can throw themselves into it with the same abandon it would take to expose your guts on the street in the heart of Tokyo. You should do the same sort of rigorous training, you know. Then you wouldn't need to go traveling."

"If I were a real painter, I could achieve that sort of state whenever I wanted."

"Well then, you should do so."

"I can't if people are counting my farts all the time."

The abbot laughs. "Well, there you are, you see. Now, that lass of Shioda's, where you're staying, young Nami, after she came back from the marriage, all sorts of things used to plague her mind, till in the end she decided to come to me for some Buddhist instruction. And now look at her, she's come a long way with it. These days she's got a fine head on her shoulders."

"Well, well, I did get the impression she was no ordinary woman."

"No, she's very sharp. A young monk studying under me by the name of Taian was led to a moment of great crisis in life on account of her, you know. It's proved to be an excellent aid to enlightenment for him, I understand."

The pine casts its shadow across the quiet garden. The distant sea glimmers faintly, with a shifting light that seems to answer and yet not answer the lights that fill the sky. The fishing boats' far lamps wink on and off.

"Look at the shadow of that pine."

"It's beautiful, isn't it?"

"Is that all?"

"Yes."

"It's not simply beautiful. It cares not if the wind blows."

I drink off the last of my tea, place the cup upside down on the tea tray, and rise to my feet.

"We'll see you as far as the gate. Ryōooneeeen! The guest is leaving!"

When we step out of the priests' quarters, the pigeons are cooing.

"There's nothing more enchanting than pigeons, you know. I have only to clap, and they all come flying over. Here, I'll show you."

The moonlight has grown brighter still. In the deep silence, the magnolia tree proffers its tangled branches of cloudy blossoms to the vault of the sky. Suddenly the abbot startles the very center of the clear spring night with a loud clap. The sound dies on the breeze, and not a single pigeon appears.

"Not coming, eh? Funny, I thought they would."

Ryōnen looks at me with a hint of a smile. The abbot appears to think pigeons can see in the dark. What a happy innocence.

At the gate we part. I turn to watch their two rounded shadows, one large and one small, follow each other back down the stone path and disappear.

CHAPTER 12

I believe it was Oscar Wilde who remarked that Christ's approach to life was supremely artistic. I don't know about Christ, but I certainly believe this statement could justly be applied to the abbot of Kankaiji. Not in the sense of tastes, or of being in accord with the times—after all, this is a man who hangs in his alcove a Bodhidharma scroll painting so execrable it scarcely deserves the name of art, and boasts about how fine it is; a man who believes that there are doctorates for painters, and who thinks that pigeons can see in the dark. But I would claim that, despite all this, he is a real artist. His heart is a bottomless well. Everything passes straight through it without hindrance. He moves freely through all places, creates at will, and moves on, and there's not the least hint of any sullying particle of experience remaining lodged within him. If just a touch of discernment and taste could be added to his brain, he would become the perfect artist, at one with whatever situation he found himself in, maintaining the artist's essential state of mind even in the most trivial everyday moments of life.

I, on the other hand, will never be an artist in the true sense as long as the detectives are still at work counting my farts. I can turn to the easel, I can take up the palette, but I cannot be a painter. Only by bringing myself to this unknown mountain village and steeping myself deep in its late spring world have I at last found within me the attitude of the pure artist. Once I have crossed this frontier, all the beauties of the earth become mine. Though no drop of paint nor jot of brushstroke ever meets the pure white canvas before me, I am nevertheless an artist of the highest order. I grant I do not equal Michelangelo in artistry, nor Raphael in skill, but my artist's soul can take its place alongside those of the great men of antiquity, proud and equal. I have not made a single painting since arriving, indeed I almost feel that to have brought the painting box along at all was a mere whim. And you call yourself a painter? you may say with a sneer. But sneer though you may, I am for the present a true artist, a magnificent artist. Those who have attained this state don't necessarily produce great works—but all who produce great works must first attain it.

These are my meditations as I savor a cigarette after breakfast. The sun has risen high above the trailing mists. I slide open the screen doors to gaze out onto the mountainside beyond. The spring green of the trees seems almost transparent in the sunlight and glows with an astonishing richness.

I've always felt that the relationship between air, form, and color is the most fascinating study that the world affords. Do you focus on color to evoke air, or on form? Or do you focus on air, and weave color and form through it? The slightest shift in approach can alter the feel of a painting in any number of ways. It will also differ, of course, depending on the tastes of the painter himself, and be limited by the strictures of time and place. The landscape paintings of the English contain no hint of brightness. Perhaps they dislike bright works, but even if this weren't the case, nothing bright could be produced in that dismal air of theirs. The paintings of the Englishman Goodall, however, are a completely different matter, and justly so.[1] Though he was English, he never painted a single English landscape. His subject was not his native land but exclusively the landscapes of Egypt and Persia, whose air is by contrast marvelously pure. Anyone seeing his paintings for the first time will be astonished at their clarity and wonder that an Englishman could produce such brilliance of color.

Nothing can be done about individual tastes, of course, but if our aim is to paint the Japanese landscape, we must depict the air and colors peculiar to it. No matter how fine you think

the colors of French paintings, you cannot simply borrow
them wholesale and claim that your painting depicts a Japanese landscape. You must immerse yourself in the natural
world, study its multifarious forms, the shifting ways of
cloud and mist, morning and evening, and only then, when
you have at last lit on the very color you need, should you
seize your tripod and rush outside to paint. Colors change
from moment to moment. If you once lose the opportunity,
you must wait a long time before your eyes fall on precisely
this color again.

The mountainside to which I now lift my gaze is flush with
a marvelous hue rarely seen in these parts. It's a great shame
to have come all this way to be confronted by this moment,
and to let it slip. Let me just try to paint it. . . .

I open the door to leave, and there at the second-floor window, leaning against the sliding paper door, stands Nami. Her
chin is buried in the collar of her kimono, and only her profile is visible. Just as I am on the point of greeting her, her
right hand rises as if lifted on a breeze, while the left hand
continues to hang at her side. Something—is it lightning?—
flashes swiftly up and down at her breast, there is a sharp
click, and the flash is gone again. In her left hand I now see
she's holding the unvarnished wooden scabbard of a dagger.
The next instant she has hidden herself behind the screen
door. I leave the inn with the illusion that I have stopped in
briefly on a morning performance at the Kabuki theater.

Turning left directly outside the gate, I'm soon confronted
with a steep path that sets off almost perpendicularly straight
up the mountainside. Cries of bush warblers echo here and
there among the trees. On my left the gentle slope that descends to the valley is planted with mandarin trees; two low
hills stand to my right, apparently also devoted entirely to
mandarin orchards. How many years ago was it that I visited
here? I can't be bothered counting. I remember it was a cold
December, and it was the first time I'd come across a landscape of hills swathed everywhere with mandarin trees like
this. I asked one of the mandarin pickers perched in a tree if I

could purchase a branch of them, and he replied cheerily, "Take as many as you want," and began to sing an odd song. Back in Tokyo, I remember reflecting wonderingly, you had to go to a herbalist to come by so much as the skin of a mandarin. I heard a frequent sound of gunshot, and when I asked what it was, I was told that hunters were out shooting ducks. On that visit I had not the faintest inkling of Nami's existence.

As an actor, she would make a marvelous female impersonator on the Kabuki stage. When most actors appear onstage, their performance is that of someone outside the home setting, but she spends her everyday life performing, and she doesn't even recognize the fact. She's a natural actor. Hers could truly be called "the artist's life." Thanks to Nami, I am well on the path to true painting.

Unless I view her behavior as performance, its unsettling nature will doubtless plague me to distraction all day. An ordinary novelist, equipped with the standard tools of reason or human sentiment, would quickly find the study of this woman overstimulating and retreat in disgust. If any emotional entanglement were to develop between us in the real world, my suffering would no doubt be unspeakable. But my aim on this journey is to leave behind the world of common emotions and achieve the transcendent state of the artist, so I must view everything before me through the lens of art— apprehending people in terms of the Noh or other drama or as figures in a poem. Viewed from my chosen artistic perspective, this woman's behavior is more aesthetically satisfying than that of any woman I have come across, and it's all the more beautiful for the fact that she is unaware of the beauty of her art.

Don't misunderstand me. I maintain that it's quite unreasonable to judge behavior such as hers simply as unbecoming in a citizen of our society. Yes, to do good, to be virtuous, to preserve chastity, to sacrifice oneself for the sake of duty are no easy matters. All who attempt these things must suffer to achieve them, and if we are to brave such suffering, somewhere must lurk the promise of a pleasure great enough to defeat the pain. Painting, poetry, drama—these are simply different names for the pleasure within this anguish. When we once grasp this truth, we will at last act with courage and grace; we will overcome all adversity and be in a position to satisfy the supreme aesthetic urges of our heart. One must disregard physical suffering, set material inconvenience at naught, cultivate a dauntless spirit, and be prepared to submit to any torture for the sake of righteousness and humanity. Defined on the narrow basis of human sentiment, Art could be said to be a bright light hidden within the heart of us men of learning, a crystallization of that fierce dedication that cannot but repel evil and cleave to the good, shrink from the warped and align itself with the straight, aid the weak and crush the strong—a crystal that will shoot back the flashing arrows of the daylight world that would pierce it.

People will laugh at someone's behavior when they see it as theatrical. They are really laughing at what is, from the point of view of human sentiment, the quite incomprehensible and meaningless sacrifice being made on the grounds of purity of aesthetic principle. They deride the folly of parading one's sensibility before the world rather than awaiting a moment that will allow innate beauty of character naturally to shine forth. Those who have a true grasp of such matters may well scoff, but the louts and riffraff who have no understanding of taste, and choose to scorn others by comparing them to their own base natures, are unforgivable. There was once a youth who leaped five hundred feet to his doom down a waterfall into the swirling rapids, leaving behind him a final poem on the rock above.[2] To me, it seems that this young man sacrificed his life, that precious gift, for the sake of beauty pure and simple. Such a death is heroic, though the impulse that prompted it is difficult for us to comprehend. But how can those who fail to grasp the heroism of that death dare to deride his action? Such people, who can never know the emotions of one who accomplishes such supreme heroism, must surely forfeit all right to scoff, for they are inferior to this young man in being unable, even in circumstances that justify such an action, to achieve his noble sacrifice.

I'm a painter and, as such, a man whose professionally cultivated sensibility would automatically put me above my more uncouth neighbors, if I were to descend to dwelling in the common world of human emotions. As a member of society, my superior position allows me to instruct others. Furthermore, the artist is capable of a greater aesthetic behavior than those who have no sense of poetry or painting, no artistic skill. In the realm of human feelings, a beautiful action is one of truth, justice, and righteousness; and to express truth, justice, and righteousness through one's behavior is to align oneself with the pattern of behavior deemed proper for civic life.

Now, I have removed myself for a while from that sphere of human feelings, and during this journey I feel no necessity to rejoin it. Were I to do so, the whole point of the journey would be lost. I must sieve from the rough sands of human emotions the pure gold that lies within and fix my eyes on that alone. For now, I choose not to play my part as a member of society but to identify myself purely and simply as a professional painter, to cut myself loose from the entangling strictures of gross self-interest, and to dedicate myself fully to my relationship with the artist's canvas—and of course my disinterested stance applies also to mountains and to water, not to mention to other people. Under the circumstances, then, I must observe Nami's behavior in the same way, simply for what it is.

When I have climbed about a quarter of a mile, a single white-walled dwelling looms up ahead. A house among the mandarin trees, I think. The road now divides in two, and I turn left, with the white-walled house off to one side. I glance back and discover a girl in a red skirt climbing the hill behind me. The skirt gives way to a pair of brown shins, below which is a pair of straw sandals, advancing steadily toward me. Petals from the mountain cherries tumble about her head. At her back she bears the shining sea.

She arrives at the top of the steep path and emerges onto the flat top of the knoll. To the north tower fold upon fold of spring's green peaks, perhaps the view that I gazed up at from my balcony this morning. To the south is what seems like a burned area about fifty yards wide, and beyond it a crumbling cliff face; below lies the mandarin orchard I have just passed through, and beyond the distant village, all that meets the eye is that familiar expanse of blue sea.

The main path has become indistinguishable among the numerous tracks that meet and part and intersect. All are a path of some sort, and none is the path itself. A further interesting confusion is the intriguing patches of dark red earth that are visible here and there in the grass, not clearly connected to this or that track.

I wander through the grass, looking for a place to settle myself down. The landscape that looked so suitable for painting when viewed from my balcony also seems suddenly to have lost its unity and coherence. Its color too is gradually fading. As I plod stupidly hither and yon in this fashion, all desire to paint deserts me. With the need to paint gone, the selection of a place no longer matters—wherever I choose to sit will become my home. The warmth of the spring sunlight has penetrated to the roots of the grass, and as I plump myself down, I sense that I am inadvertently crushing beneath me an invisible shimmer of heat haze.

Down beyond my feet shines the sea. The utterly cloudless spring sky casts its sunlight over the entire sea surface, imparting a warmth that suggests the sunlight has penetrated deep within its waves. A swath of delicate Prussian blue spreads lengthwise across it, and here and there an intricate play of colors swims over a layering of fine white-gold scales. Between the vastness of the spring sunlight that shines upon the world, and the vastness of the water that brims beneath it, the only visible thing is a single white sail no bigger than a little fingernail. The sail is absolutely motionless. Those ships that plied these waters in days gone by, bearing tributes from afar, must have looked like this. Apart from the sail, heaven and earth consist entirely of the world of shining sunlight and the world of sunlit sea.

I throw myself back onto the grass. My hat slips from my forehead and haloes my head. The grass is studded with little clumps of wild japonica bush one or two feet tall, and my face has come to rest just in front of one. Japonica is an interesting plant. Its branches obstinately refuse to bend, yet neither are they straight: each small straight twig collides with another small straight twig at an angle, so that the whole branch consists of a series of obliques, tranquilly ornamented with rather pointless scarlet or white flowers, and a casual scattering of soft leaves to top it off. You could characterize the japonica as belonging to the type of the enlightened fool. Some in this world doggedly retain an awkward and innocent honesty—they will be reborn as japonica. It's the flower that I myself would like to become.

When I was a child, I once cut myself some twigs of japonica, complete with flowers and leaves, and arranged them attractively to make a rack for holding my writing brush. In it I propped a cheap, soft-haired brush, and seeing the contraption there before me on my desk, the white brush head peeping out from among the flowers and leaves, gave me great pleasure. When I went to bed that night, the japonica brush rack filled my thoughts. As soon as I awoke the next morning, I leaped from my bed and ran to the desk—to discover the flowers drooping and the leaves dried. Only the brush head glowed there unaltered in their midst. That such a beautiful thing could wither and die in the space of a single night appalled me. This earlier self seems to me now enviably unsullied by the world.

The japonica that meets my eyes now, as soon as I lie back, is an old and intimate friend. As I gaze at it, my mind drifts pleasantly, and the impulse to poetry wells up in me again.

Lying here, I ponder, and as each line of a Chinese poem comes to me, I jot it down in my sketchbook. After a little time, the poem seems complete. I reread it from the beginning.

> Beset by thoughts I leave my gate.
> The spring breeze stirs my robes.
> Fragrant herbs have sprung in the wheel ruts.
> The derelict track leads on into mists.
> I halt and gaze about me.
> All is aglow with light.
> I hear bush warblers at their song
> And in my eyes are drifting cherry blossoms.
> "At the road's end a vast plain unfolds"—
> I write this line on an old temple's door.
> The lone walker's solitude fills the sky.
> A single wild goose wings homeward through
>   the heavens.
> What subtleties lie within one small heart!
> Right and wrong—forgotten in this eternal
>   moment.
> Poised at thirty on the edge of old age
> Yet now a soft spring light wraps me about.
> Wandering thus, at one with nature's changes,
> I calmly breathe the fragrance all about.[3]

That's it! I've done it! I've truly captured the feeling of lying here gazing at the japonica, all worldly thoughts forgotten. It doesn't matter if the poem doesn't actually include the japonica, or the sea, as long as the feeling comes through. I give a groan of pleasure—and am astonished to hear the sound of a human clearing his throat not far from me.

Rolling over, I peer in the direction of the voice. A man comes around the edge of the flat knoll and emerges from among the trees.

His eyes are visible beneath the tilted rim of a dilapidated brown felt hat. I can't make them out in detail, but they are evidently shifting uneasily. He is dressed rather indeterminately in an indigo-striped garment tucked up at the thighs, and bare feet in high clogs. The wild beard suggests he is one of those roaming mountain monks.

I assume he'll proceed on down the steep mountain path,

KUSAMAKURA

but to my surprise he turns back at the edge and retraces his steps. Instead of disappearing back the way he came, however, he changes direction yet again. No one could be wandering to and fro on this grassy flat unless he were here to take a stroll, surely. Yet this is hardly the figure of a mere stroller; nor would such a person be living hereabouts. The man pauses in his tracks from time to time, tilting his head questioningly, gazing all about him. He appears to be deep in thought. Perhaps he's waiting for someone. I can't make it out at all.

My eyes are held by this alarming fellow. I'm not particularly afraid; nor do I feel tempted to draw him; it's simply that my eyes are glued to him. My gaze continues to travel left and right, following his movements, until suddenly he comes to a standstill—and then another human figure appears in the scene.

They seem to recognize each other, and both approach. Watching them, my vision gradually focuses in on a single point in the middle of the grassy flat. Now these two figures come together face-to-face, with the spring mountains behind them and the spring sea before.

One, the man, is of course my wild mountain monk. And the other? The other is a woman—Nami.

As soon as I recognize her, this morning's image of her holding the dagger returns to me. Could it be hidden in her robes now? I wonder, and for all my vaunted "nonemotional" stance, I shudder.

Facing each other, the two maintain their pose for a long moment. There is no hint of movement in either figure. Perhaps their mouths are moving, but no voices reach me. At length the man hangs his head, and the woman turns toward the mountains. I cannot see her face.

There in the mountains a bush warbler sings; the woman appears to listen to it. After a while the man raises his deeply bowed head and half-turns on his heels. Something odd is happening. The woman rapidly breaks her pose and turns to face the sea. Something peeps from her waistband—it must be that dagger. Head triumphantly high, the man begins to leave.

The woman takes two steps in pursuit of him. She is wearing straw sandals. He pauses—has she called him? As he turns, her right hand goes to her waist. Watch out!

What she produces is not the dagger I anticipate, however, but a cloth object like a purse of money. Her white hand holds it out toward him, a long string swaying below it in the spring breeze.

One foot placed before her, the body bent slightly from the waist, the extended white hand and wrist, and that purple cloth bag—this image is all I need for a picture.

The composition, with its dash of purple, is beautifully connected by the perfect balance of the man's turned body a few inches away. Distant yet close—that expression could have been made to fit this moment. The woman's figure seems to draw him toward her, the man's seems drawn backward by her, yet these forces are merely notional. The relationship between them is cleanly broken by the edge of the proffered purple bag.

The interest of the picture is intensified by the fact that the delicate balance these two figures maintain is set against the clear contrast in their faces and clothes.

This swarthy, thickset, bearded man; that delicate form, with her long neck and sloping shoulders and firm, clear features. This wild figure twisted harshly toward her; that elegant shape, sleekly graceful even in her everyday kimono, leaning gently forward from the waist. His misshapen brown hat and indigo-striped garment tucked to the thigh; her elegant curve of hair, combed to a gossamer glint, and the captivating glimpse of padding deep within the glowing black satin of her obi folds—all this is marvelous material for a picture.

The man puts out his hand and takes the purse, and at once the beautifully balanced tension in their mutual poses disintegrates; the woman's figure ceases to draw him, while he in turn has broken free of that force. Painter though I am, I have never before realized just how powerfully psychological states can influence a picture's composition.

They move apart now, to left and right. No tension holds the two figures in relation, and the composition has lost all vestige of coherence. At the entrance to the wood the man pauses and turns to look back, but the woman never glances behind her. She is walking smoothly toward me. At length she arrives directly in front of me.

"Sir!" she exclaims, and again, "Sir!"

Damn! When did she notice me?

"What is it?" I inquire, poking my head up above the japonica. My hat tumbles back onto the grass behind me.

"What are you doing there?"

"I was lying here composing a poem."

"Liar! You saw what happened just now, didn't you?"

"Just now? You mean, you two. . . . Yes, I did see a bit."

She laughs. "You didn't need to just see a bit. You could have watched all of it, you know."

"To tell the truth, I did see quite a lot."

"There you are, then! Come on over here a moment. Come out from under that japonica."

I meekly do as instructed.

"Was there something else you wanted to do there?"

"No, I was just thinking of heading back."

"Well then, let's go together."

"Very well."

Still submissive, I return to the clump of japonica, put on my hat, retrieve my painting equipment, and set off to walk beside her.

"Did you paint anything?"

"No, I gave up."

"You haven't painted a single picture since you've been here, have you?"

"That's so, yes."

"But surely it's odd coming here specially to paint and then producing nothing?"

"There are no odds about it."

"Really? Why not?"

"What's the odds whether I paint a picture or not, after all?"

"That's a pun, isn't it." She laughs. "You're very nonchalant, I must say."

"What's the point of coming to a place like this if you're not going to be nonchalant?"

"Oh, come now. No matter what place you're in, being alive has no point unless you're nonchalant. Look at me, I'm not at all embarrassed to have been seen as you saw me back there."

"There's no need to be embarrassed, surely."

"You think so? So who do you imagine that man was?"

"Hmm. Well, he certainly isn't someone with a lot of money."

She laughs again. "A good guess. You're a master of insight, aren't you! Actually, he has so little money he can't stay in the country, and he came to get some money from me."

"Really? Where did he come from?"

"He came from the town down there."

"That's a long way. And where is he going?"

"Well, it seems he's going to Manchuria."

"What will he do there?"

"What will he do there? I don't know, he may make some money, or he may die."

I raise my eyes to look at her. The little smile that has been hovering on her lips is rapidly disappearing. I can't guess the meaning of her words.

"That man is my husband."

Quick as a flash, she has landed me a slashing blow! I'm utterly caught by surprise. I had of course had no intention of asking who he was; nor had I expected her to expose herself to me like this.

"How was that? Did I surprise you?" she said.

"Yes, you did a bit."

"He's not my present husband. He's the one I had to sever relations with."

"I see. So . . ."

"So nothing. That's all."

"I see. . . . That fine white-walled house over there in the mandarin orchard, it's in a nice place, isn't it? Whose house is it?"

"That's my older brother's house. Let's call there on the way home."

"Do you have some business there?"

"Yes, he's asked me to do something."

"I'll come with you, then."

When we reach the beginning of the path down the mountainside, we don't descend but turn right and, after a climb of a little over a hundred yards, arrive at the front gate of the house. Rather than proceeding straight to the entrance, we go to the garden at one side. Nami strides boldly along, so I follow suit. Three or four palms stand in the south-facing garden. Immediately beyond the earth wall, the mandarin orchard begins.

Without preliminaries, Nami seats herself on the edge of the veranda and remarks, "It's a fine view. Look."

"Yes, it certainly is."

Behind the sliding doors to the house, all is quiet. Nothing suggests anyone is home. Nami shows no sign of calling on anyone. She simply sits at her ease, gazing down at the slope of mandarin orchard beyond. I feel rather puzzled. What business has actually brought her here?

Our conversation has petered out, and we sit on in silence, looking at the mandarin trees. The noonday sun floods the mountain with its warm rays, and the mandarin leaves that fill our vision seem to steam and glitter. After a while a cock crows loudly in the barn behind the house.

"Good heavens, it's noon!" Nami exclaims. "I was forgetting what I had to do. Kyūichi! Kyūichi!" She reaches over and slides open the door with a slight clatter. I can see a large empty room; a pair of scrolls in the style of the Kanō School hang somehow mournfully in the alcove.[4]

"Kyūichi!"

At last an answering voice is heard from the barn. The

approaching steps pause behind the sliding door. It opens, and in an instant the dagger in its white wooden sheath is tumbling over the matting.

"A farewell gift from your uncle for you!" Nami announces.

I had no inkling of the moment when her hand went to her waistband. The dagger somersaults two or three times, then slides smoothly across the matting to Kyūichi's feet. It has slipped a little from the loose sheath, to reveal an inch or so of cold glinting steel.

CHAPTER 13

It is the day of Kyūichi's departure. We are accompanying him by boat down the river as far as Yoshida Station. Besides Kyūichi, our boat contains Mr. Shioda, Nami, her brother, Genbei, and myself, of course merely in the capacity of invitee.

I am happy to go along as "invitee"—indeed, I am happy to go along without puzzling over reasons and roles at all. Prudence, after all, can play no part in the "nonemotional" journey.

Our boat is a flat-bottomed one, rather like a raft with sides added. The old man is seated in the middle, Nami and myself in the stern, and Kyūichi and Nami's brother in the bow. Genbei sits apart, looking after the luggage.

"Kyūichi, how do you feel about war?" Nami inquires. "Do you like it?"

"I won't know till I'm in it. There'll be suffering, I should think, but perhaps there'll be pleasures too" is his innocent reply.

"No matter the suffering," the old gentleman remarks, "it's for the sake of the nation."

Nami's next question is equally odd. "Surely you're inclined to go to war and see what it's all about, now that you've been given a dagger?"

"Yes, I guess so," Kyūichi responds with a light nod. The old gentleman laughs and tugs at his beard. His son pretends to have heard nothing.

Nami now abruptly thrusts her pale face close to Kyūichi and demands, "How are you going to be able to fight with that sort of nonchalant attitude?"

"You'd make a fine soldier, Nami," says her brother. These are the first words he has spoken to her. His tone indicates that the remark is not intended as a joke.

"Me? Me, a soldier? If I could become a soldier, I'd have done it long ago. I'd be dead by now. Kyūichi, you must die too. You'll lose your honor if you come home alive."

"Good heavens, hold your tongue!" exclaims her father. "No, no, you must return in triumph. Death is not the only way to serve one's nation. I plan to live a couple of years yet. We'll be able to meet again." The old man's last drawn-out words tremble and are lost in tears; only the imperative of manliness prevents him from spilling all that is in his heart. Kyūichi says nothing but simply sits with his head turned aside, looking at the riverbank.

There's a large willow on the bank, and beneath it sits a man in a little boat moored to the tree, staring at his fishing line. As our boat goes by, trailing its rocking wake, the man glances up, and his eyes meet Kyūichi's. No acknowledging charge flows between the two. The man's mind is focused on his fishing, while Kyūichi's busy thoughts have no space for so much as a single fish. Our boat floats calmly on past the unknown fisherman.

If you were to stand in the middle of the street, as a streetcar director does, at the approach to Tokyo's Nihonbashi Bridge, and stop every one of the hundreds who pass by every minute and learn each one's trials and troubles, this world of ours would seem to you an appallingly difficult place in which to live. We humans meet and part as strangers—if this were not so, who would be willing to take on the job of standing there directing the milling streetcars? It's a lucky thing that our unknown fisherman seeks no explanation for Kyūichi's tearful face. When I turn back to look, he is calmly watching his float. He'll likely go on sitting there, gazing at that float, until the Russian War is over.

The river is shallow and quite narrow; the current flows gently. Our boat slips along through the water, moving inexorably on and on through the passing spring toward some other place, a place full of noisy people who love to collide with one another. This young man with the brutal mark of bloodshed upon his brow is drawing us mercilessly along with him. The bonds of fate are compelling him to a dark and fearsome land far to the north, and we whose fate is tangled with his are likewise compelled to travel with him until the ties that bind us at last give way. When this happens, something between us will audibly snap; he alone will be reeled inescapably in by the hand of his own fate, while we in turn are fated to remain behind. Beg and struggle though we might, he will be powerless to draw us with him.

It is delightful how gently the boat floats on. Those must be field horsetails covering either bank; farther up are stands of willows. Here and there among them a low farmhouse reveals a thatched roof and a glimpse of a sooty window; occasionally a few white geese spill forth and waddle cackling into the river.

That flash of brightness between those willows must be a white peach tree in bloom. A loom knocks and clatters, and from within its rhythm the sound of a woman's plangent singing drifts across the water; the song is impossible to recognize.

"Would you do a portrait of me?" Nami suddenly says to me. Kyūichi and her brother are deep in military talk, and the old man has nodded off.

"Certainly," I say obligingly. Taking out my sketchbook, I jot down the following poem and pass it to her:

> That silken obi
> unraveled by the breeze of spring—
> what name does it bear?

She laughs. "It's no good just dashing something off like this. You must put a bit of care into it, and do something that reveals my temperament."

"I've been wanting to do the same thing myself, but somehow that face of yours just won't compose itself into a picture the way it is."

"That's a charming answer, I must say! So what should I do to get a picture?"

"Oh, I could do one right now. It's just that there's something lacking. It would be a shame to draw you without it."

"What do you mean, lacking? It's the face I was born with, so there's nothing I can do about it."

"The face one's born with can change in all manner of ways."

"You mean I can change it?"

"Yes."

"Don't treat me like a fool just because I'm a woman."

"On the contrary, it's because you're a woman that you say foolish things like that."

"Well then, let's see you make some changes to your own face."

"It already changes quite enough from day to day."

She falls silent and turns away. The riverbanks are now level with the water, and the flat expanse of unplanted rice fields beyond is deep in flowering milk vetch. A vast sea of flowers stretches away forever, blurred with the haze of spring so that it seems a recent rain has half-dissolved those vivid dots of red and run them all together. Looking up, I see the towering form of a steep peak half-blocking the sky, with a wisp of spring cloud spilled out across its flank.

"That's the mountain you crossed." Nami extends a white hand over the side of the boat and points to the dreamlike peak.

"Is Tengu Rock around there?"

"See that patch of purple below the dark green part?"

"That shadowy bit?"

"Is it shadow? It looks like a bald patch to me."

"Come now, it's a hollow. If it was bald, it would have more brown in it."

"Is that so? Anyway, Tengu Rock is apparently in behind that."

"So the Seven Bends would be a little farther to the left, then."

"They're way off somewhere else, on a mountain behind that one."

"Ah yes, that's true. But I'd guess they're about where that bit of cloud is hanging."

"Yes, that's the direction."

At this point the elbow of the old man slips from the edge of the boat where he's propped it to doze, and he awakens with a start.

"Not there yet?"

He stretches, chest out, right elbow drawn back, left arm thrust straight before him, then does an imitation of releasing an arrow from the bow. Nami chuckles.

"Don't mind me, it's a habit of mine."

I too laugh. "I see you like archery," I remark.

"I could draw a good thick bow in my youth," he replies, patting his left shoulder, "and even now my left-hand action is still remarkably steady."

Up in the bow, the talk of war is in full swing.

At length, the boat enters a townscape. I notice a sign painted on the low paper window of a little bar, "Drinks and Snacks," and farther on an old-fashioned tavern. We pass a lumberyard. Occasionally the sound of a rickshaw comes from the road beyond. Swallows twist and twitter in the air; geese honk.

Now our little party leaves the boat, and we make our way to the station.

We are being dragged yet deeper into the real world, which I define as the world that contains trains. Nothing can be more quintessentially representative of twentieth-century civilization than the steam train. It roars along, packed tight with hundreds of people in the one box, merciless in its progress, and all those hundreds crammed in there must travel at the same speed, stop at the same places, and submit to a baptismal submersion in the same swirling steam. Some say that people "ride" in a train, but I would say they are thrust into it; some speak of "going" by train, but it seems to me they are transported by it. Nothing is more disdainful of individuality. Having expended all its means to develop the individual, civilization then proceeds to crush it by all possible means. Present civilization gives each person his little patch of earth and tells him he may wake and sleep as he pleases on it—but then it throws up an iron railing around it, and threatens us with dire consequences if we should put a foot outside this barrier. Those who can act as they please in their own little patch naturally feel the urge to do the same beyond it, so the pitiful citizens of this world spend their days biting and raging at the boundary fence that hems them in. Civilization, having given individuals their freedom and turned them into wild beasts thereby, then maintains the peace by throwing these unfortunates behind bars. This isn't real peace, it's the peace of the zoo, where the tiger lies in his cage glaring out at the gaping sightseers. Should one bar of that cage come loose, the world would fall apart. Then we will have our second French Revolution. Indeed, the revolution is already under way night and day among individuals; the great European playwright Ibsen has provided us with detailed examples of the conditions necessary for it to occur. I must say, whenever I see one of those fierce trains hurtling along, treating all on board indiscriminately as so much freight, and mentally balance the individuals crammed in there against the train's utter disregard for their individuality—I can only say, Watch out, this could be nasty if you're not careful! Modern civilization in fact reeks of such dangers. The steam train hurtling blindly into the darkness ahead is simply one of them.

I sit in a tea shop at the station, staring thoughtfully at the piece of cake before me as I ponder this train theory of mine. I can't very well write it down in my sketchbook, and I feel no need to talk to anyone about it, so I simply sit here in silence, eating my cake and drinking my tea.

Opposite me are two men. Both wear straw sandals, one has a red blanket over his shoulders, and the other is dressed in pale green workman's trousers with patches at the knees, to which he presses his hands.

"No good, eh?"

"No good."

"We oughta have two stomachs, eh, like a cow."

"That'd be the answer. One goes wrong, you just cut it out."

This country fellow is apparently suffering from stomach problems. The stench blowing from the Manchurian battlefields has not reached these men's nostrils; nor do they understand the evils of modern civilization. They know nothing of such matters as revolution; indeed, they haven't so much as heard the word. They're still at the stage where they can seriously entertain the possibility of having two stomachs. I take out my sketchbook and set about sketching the two figures.

A bell begins to clang. The ticket is already bought.

"Right, let's go," says Nami, rising to her feet.

The old man stands with a grunt of effort. Our party goes through the ticket gate and out onto the platform. The bell is ringing fiercely.

With a roar, the serpent of civilization comes slowly writhing along the glittering tracks, belching black smoke from its jaws.

"So the time has come to say farewell," says the old man.

"Take good care of yourself," Kyūichi responds with a bow.

"Make sure you come home dead," Nami says once more.

"Is the luggage here?" asks her brother.

The serpent draws to a halt in front of us. The doors along its side open, and now people are streaming in and out. Kyūichi boards, leaving the old man, his son, Nami, and myself standing there outside.

With a single turn of those wheels, Kyūichi will be no longer of our world. He is off to a world far distant, where men labor amid the reek of gunpowder, and slither and fall on a red slick, while the sky thunders ceaselessly above. Kyūichi, already on his way there, stands wordlessly in the carriage gazing out at us. Here is the snapping point of our mutual fates—his that has drawn us down from the mountains, and ours that have been drawn along by him. The break is already happening, for all that the carriage doors and windows are still open, our faces are still visible to each other, and a mere six feet separate him who is leaving from us who remain behind.

The conductor comes running down the platform toward us, clapping the doors shut one by one, and as each closes, the distance between the travelers and those who stay behind increases. Finally Kyūichi's door slams shut. There are now two worlds. The old man steps closer to the window, and the young man thrusts his head out.

"Careful, it's moving!" comes a cry, and already the train is heartlessly chugging into motion. One after another the windows slide past us. Kyūichi's face grows small.

Then as the last third-class carriage is passing me, another face appears at the window. Gazing disconsolately out is the bearded visage of the wild mountain monk, under his brown felt hat. His eyes and Nami's suddenly find each other. The chugging train is picking up speed, and in another instant the wild face is gone. Standing there in a daze, Nami continues to stare after it, and astonishingly, her face is flooded with an emotion that I have never until this moment witnessed there—pitying love.

"That's it! That's it! That's what I need for the picture!" I murmur, patting her on the shoulder. At last, with this moment, the canvas within my own heart has found its full and final form.

Notes

CHAPTER 1

1. *By my eastern hedge:* A verse from the poem "Drinking Wine," by the Chinese poet Tao Yuanming (365–427), a work famous for extolling the natural world and the calm heart divorced from the troubles of human life.
2. *Seated alone:* A verse from the poem "House in the Bamboo Village" by the Chinese poet Wang Wei (699–759).
3. Hototogisu *or* Konjikiyasha: *Hototogisu,* written by Sōseki's contemporary Tokutomi Roka (1868–1927), depicts the tragedy of a tubercular woman separated from her beloved husband by her feudalistic family. *Konjikiyasha,* by another contemporary, Ozaki Kōyō (1867–1903), also depicts the sorrows of love. Both novels were immensely popular.
4. *no more do they . . . peace and tranquillity:* In Chinese legend a fisherman takes his boat upstream and wanders into a grove of flowering plums. There he discovers the tranquil realm of the Taoist sages, which has no contact with the mundane world.
5. Shichikiochi *or* Sumidagawa: *Shichikiochi* is an anonymous Noh play that dramatizes the story of a loyal retainer prepared to sacrifice his child to save his master. The Noh play *Sumidagawa,* by Zeami (c.1364–c.1443), portrays a woman crazed by grief at the abduction of her child; she travels to the distant river Sumida in search of him.
6. *Bashō . . . composed a haiku on it:* Bashō (1644–94), the famous Edo-period haiku poet, wrote this haiku: "Plagued by fleas and lice—/and here is my horse peeing/right by the pillow."
7. *haori:* A *haori* is a short coat worn over Japanese dress.

CHAPTER 2

1. *a Hōshō School production of the Noh play* Takasago: Hōshō, one of the five schools of Noh performance, had its theater in the Kanda district of Tokyo. *Takasago,* by Zeami, is one of the most famous Noh plays. Its protagonists are an old couple who are the spirits of two pine trees.

2. *bush warblers:* These birds have a sweet call that poetically evokes spring.

3. *the mountain crone of Rosetsu's painting:* A famous painting by the Edo-period painter Nagasawa Rosetsu (1754–99) depicts the mythic wild-haired old woman of the mountains (*ya-mamba*).

4. *the war:* The Russo-Japanese War of 1904–5.

5. *in Izen's ears:* Hirose Izen (1652?–1711) was a disciple of the haiku poet Bashō. He spent much time on journeys composing.

6. *Suzuka's far pass:* Suzuka Mountain is on the border between present-day Mie and Shiga prefectures. The Suzuka Pass was renowned as a difficult place on the old Tōkaidō road between Kyoto and Edo (Tokyo) and often appeared in travel poems.

7. *it is not in fact my own poem:* Sōseki's friend the poet Masaoka Shiki (1867–1902) wrote a haiku that differs in only one word.

8. *the* takashimada *style:* an elaborate high coiffure worn by a bride.

9. *Ophelia in Millais's painting:* The English painter John Everett Millais (1829–96), in his famous *Ophelia,* depicted her floating down a river among flowers. Although Sōseki describes the hands as folded, they are not so in the painting.

10. *As the autumn's dew . . . this brief world:* A poem found in the ancient poetry collection *Manyōshū* (mid-eighth century) was said to be composed by a girl torn between two lovers. The legend told here is a local variation loosely based on this story.

11. *the magic feather cloak . . . demand that I return it:* In the Noh play *Hagoromo* (*The Feather Cloak*), based on a folk legend, a fisherman finds an angel's feather cloak cast aside on a beach while she bathes, but he returns it to her when she pleads that she cannot fly back to heaven without it.

CHAPTER 3

1. *Bōshū province:* In the southern part of present-day Chiba prefecture.
2. *"Bamboo shadows..."*: This quotation comes from a well-known collection of epigrammatic sayings, *Taigentan,* by sixteenth-century writer Hong Zieheng.
3. *Kōsen ... Mokuan:* These seventeenth-century priests of the Ōbaku sect were renowned for their calligraphy.
4. *Jakuchū:* Itō Jakuchū (1716–1800) was famous for his paintings of creatures and plants.
5. *an Ōkyo gives us the beauty of a ghost:* Maruyama Ōkyo (1733–95) famously painted the ghost of a woman in diaphanous robes.
6. *Salvator Rosa:* Rosa (1615–73) was an artist and poet who specialized in dramatic scenes.
7. *too many season words:* A haiku must have one word associated with a season. "Blossom" and "hazy" are both season words for spring.
8. *Inari's fox god:* The Inari god is often represented by its guardian foxes. The fox is traditionally reputed to be a shape-changer, often taking the form of a woman.
9. *The fierce sculptures ... Hokusai:* Unkei (c.1148–1223) was a Buddhist sculptor. His sculptures of guardian gods at the Nara temples of Tōdaiji and Kōfukuji are among his greatest works. Hokusai (1760–1849) was a famous artist of the ukiyo-e style. His cartoon sketches of everyday life are full of movement.

CHAPTER 4

1. *Hakuin's sermons ... The Tales of Ise:* Hakuin (1685–1768) is one of the most famous Japanese Zen masters. *The Tales of Ise* (c.877–c.940) is among the earliest classic works of Japanese literature.
2. *Young Yoshitsune ... under the hazed moon:* According to legend, the folk hero Minamoto Yoshitsune (1159–89) as a youth disguised himself as a woman to make a surprise attack on the great warrior Benkei.
3. *"vast empty mountains, no one to be seen":* This is the first line of a poem in praise of the hermit's life, by Wang Wei (699–759), titled "Deer Park."
4. *"Willow Branch" Kannon bodhisattva:* Kannon, bodhisattva of

mercy, is sometimes depicted holding a willow branch, symbolizing her ability to bend and hear all prayers.

5. *"the eye is the finest thing in the human form"*: A quotation from Confucius. The eye is considered good because it unfailingly reveals a person's good or evil nature.

6. *Sadder . . . from my sight:* This poem is contained in *The Shaving of Shagpat: An Arabian Entertainment,* a novel by the British novelist George Meredith (1828–1909). The two lines below continue this poem.

7. *Rikyū:* Sen Rikyū (1522–91) first refined the rituals surrounding the drinking of whisked green tea, which subsequently developed into the modern tea ceremony.

8. *as the famous haiku has it:* This passage contains quotations from two haiku. The first is by Kikaku (1661–1707): "The bush warbler/flings his body upside down/with his first song of spring." The second is by Yosa Buson (1716–83): "The bush warbler/oh how he sings/small mouth open wide!"

CHAPTER 5

1. *Fukurokuju:* One of the seven "gods of fortune," of Chinese origin. Fukurokuju is characterized by a very elongated head. Childless couples could pray to a chosen deity in hopes of receiving the gift of a child from him.

2. *Anglo-Japanese Alliance:* In 1902 England and Japan drew up a military alliance. It was celebrated in Japan by the issue of sets of tiny crossed flags of the two nations.

CHAPTER 6

1. *Wen Tong's bamboo . . . the human figures of Buson:* Wen Tong (1018–79) was a Chinese ink painter famed for his bamboo. Unkoku Tōgan (1547–1618) was a bold and expressive painter of screens. Taigadō (Ike Taiga, 1723–76) painted in the style of the Southern School of Chinese painting known as Nanga. Yosa Buson (1716–83) was a haiku poet and painter in the Nanga style.

2. *Sesshū:* Sesshū (1420–1506) was an ink painter of landscapes.

3. *Lessing:* Gotthold Lessing (1729–81) was a German dramatist and essayist who wrote on the theory of aesthetics, most famously in *Laocoön.*

CHAPTER 8

1. *the Nansō School:* Nansō was a style of traditional ink painting originating in China.
2. *Mokubei:* Aoki Mokubei (1767–1833) was a well-known Kyoto ceramicist and ink painter.
3. *Sanyō:* Rai Sanyō (1780–1832) was a Confucian scholar and aesthete, as was his father, Shunsui (1746–1816).
4. *Tankei:* Tankei is an area of China that gave its name to the ink stones produced from its prized stone. The stone was characterized by round red spots known as shrike spots.
5. *Kyōhei:* Rai Kyōhei (1756–1834) was a disciple of Shunsui.
6. *Sorai:* Ogyū Sorai (1666–1728) was a Confucian scholar and poet.
7. *Kōtaku:* Hosoi Kōtaku (1658–1735) was a Confucian scholar and calligrapher.

CHAPTER 9

1. *"The woman emanated . . . his veins":* A free translation of a scene at the end of Chapter 8 of *Beauchamp's Career* by the English novelist George Meredith (1828–1909).

CHAPTER 10

1. *the Iwasakis and Mitsuis of this world:* The Iwasaki family, founders of the Mitsubishi Company, and the Mitsui family, founders of the Mitsui Company, were the two great financial families of the Meiji period.
2. *Timon of Athens:* This famously misanthropic Greek ruler (fifth century B.C.) was portrayed in Shakespeare's 1623 play of that name.

CHAPTER 11

1. *Iwasa Matabei:* Matabei (1578–1650) was a Japanese painter with a quirky, freestyle form.
2. *nembutsu:* A repeated chant invoking Amida Buddha. An early form of *nembutsu* worship included dance.
3. *Chao Buzhi:* Buzhi (1053–1110) was a Chinese poet, painter, and scholar. The following quotation is from *Traveling to the Northern Mountains of Xincheng*.

CHAPTER 12

1. *Goodall:* Frederick Goodall (1822–1904) was a British portraitist and landscape painter.
2. *There was once a youth . . . on the rock above:* In 1903, at the age of eighteen, Fujimura Misao, a disciple of Sōseki, committed suicide at the Kegon Falls in Nikko. He left a final poem on a nearby tree.
3. *Beset by thoughts . . . all about:* A poem composed by Sōseki in March 1899, contemporaneously with the period of his life on which this novel is based.
4. *in the style of the Kanō School:* Kanō was an elegant painting style dating from the fifteenth century.

THE STORY OF PENGUIN CLASSICS

Before 1946 . . . "Classics" are mainly the domain of academics and students; readable editions for everyone else are almost unheard of. This all changes when a little-known classicist, E. V. Rieu, presents Penguin founder Allen Lane with the translation of Homer's *Odyssey* that he has been working on in his spare time.

1946 Penguin Classics debuts with *The Odyssey*, which promptly sells three million copies. Suddenly, classics are no longer for the privileged few.

1950s Rieu, now series editor, turns to professional writers for the best modern, readable translations, including Dorothy L. Sayers's *Inferno* and Robert Graves's unexpurgated *Twelve Caesars*.

1960s The Classics are given the distinctive black covers that have remained a constant throughout the life of the series. Rieu retires in 1964, hailing the Penguin Classics list as "the greatest educative force of the twentieth century."

1970s A new generation of translators swells the Penguin Classics ranks, introducing readers of English to classics of world literature from more than twenty languages. The list grows to encompass more history, philosophy, science, religion, and politics.

1980s The Penguin American Library launches with titles such as *Uncle Tom's Cabin*, and joins forces with Penguin Classics to provide the most comprehensive library of world literature available from any paperback publisher.

1990s The launch of Penguin Audiobooks brings the classics to a listening audience for the first time, and in 1999 the worldwide launch of the Penguin Classics website extends their reach to the global online community.

The 21st Century Penguin Classics are completely redesigned for the first time in nearly twenty years. This world-famous series now consists of more than 1300 titles, making the widest range of the best books ever written available to millions—and constantly redefining what makes a "classic."

The Odyssey continues . . .

The best books ever written

PENGUIN ㉟ CLASSICS

SINCE 1946

Find out more at www.penguinclassics.com

Visit www.vpbookclub.com

CLICK ON A CLASSIC
www.penguinclassics.com

The world's greatest literature at your fingertips

Constantly updated information on more than a thousand titles,
from Icelandic sagas to ancient Indian epics, Russian drama to
Italian romance, American greats to African masterpieces

•

The latest news on recent additions to the list, updated
editions, and specially commissioned translations

•

Original essays by leading writers

•

A wealth of background material, including biographies
of every classic author from Aristotle to Zamyatin, plot
synopses, readers' and teachers' guides, useful Web links

•

Online desk and examination copy assistance for academics

•

Trivia quizzes, competitions, giveaways, news on
forthcoming screen adaptations